Wanton

A Curvy Girl Mafia Romance

Nichole Rose

Nichole Rose

Copyright © 2023 by Nichole Rose

All rights reserved. This book or any portion thereof may not be reproduced or used in any manner whatsoever without the express written permission of the author except for the use of brief quotations in a book review.

All characters appearing in this work are fictitious. Any resemblance to real persons, living or dead, is purely coincidental.

Cover by Kevin at Timeless Designs

Contents

Dedication	1
About the Book	2
Prologue	5
Chapter One	10
Chapter Two	23
Chapter Three	36
Chapter Four	51
Chapter Five	63
Chapter Six	76
Chapter Seven	89
Chapter Eight	99
Chapter Nine	114
Chapter Ten	125
Chapter Eleven	135

Chapter Twelve	141
Epilogue	147
Author's Note	152
Snow's Prince	153
Nichole's Book Beauties	155
Instalove Book Club	156
Follow Nichole	157
More By Nichole Rose	159
About Nichole Rose	164

Dedication

To BG, who gets no credit for this one because she slept through all the writing parts. But she did wake up for all the snack breaks. #doglife

About the Book

Falling for the enemy wasn't part of Luca Valentino's plan. But one taste of his curvy captive will change everything for this mafia boss.

Luca

A life in hell was the sacrifice I made to keep my brothers alive.

There's nothing I won't do to see that job through.

Even if it means seducing the enemy.

But I never intended to fall for Callandria Genovese.

She was supposed to be a means to an end, nothing more.

Now, I've got more to lose than ever.

And the woman who holds the key to my future is in chains in my bedroom.

I need her trust. I want her heart.

One way or another, I will have both.

Callandria

I've been taught to hate the Valentino family since I could walk.

I know they killed my grandfather.

But no one warned me that the real monster of the bunch was Luca.

They didn't tell me I'd find myself imprisoned in his bed, either.

Or that I'd be so reluctant to leave it.

But that's precisely what happened.

Little by little, he's slipping beneath my defenses and making me feel things I shouldn't.

But which side of him is real?

The wanton man who sets me ablaze...or the ruthless mobster who refuses to let me go?

If you like your OTT possessive older men morally gray and your curvy heroines strong, prepare to fall for Luca and Callandria in this extra steamy short mafia romance. As always, Nichole Rose books come complete with a guaranteed HEA. Safe read. No cliffhanger. Each book in the Ruined

Trilogy features a different Valentino brother and can be read as a standalone story.

Prologue

CALLANDRIA

I toss my phone on my bed, cinching my robe tightly around my waist. It's after three in the morning, but sleep alludes me like usual. This house is too much like a prison. I may be free to come and go as I please, but I'm in shackles, nonetheless. They locked into place around my ankles before I was even born.

It comes with the territory when you're a Genovese. My grandfather, Tommaso, is one of the most infamous mobsters in Chicago. My father is in just as deep as he is. So is my older brother. The fact that I'm female didn't spare me. If anything, it bound me even tighter. I may not have taken the vow of *Omertà* like they did, but I'm no freer than my brother, Marcello. I'm a *principessa*. Every moment of my life has been carefully mapped out and planned.

I've known since I was a little girl that a career of my own was out of the question. I found out when I was thirteen that love and college weren't in the cards for me, either. It was a bitter pill to swallow. It's been eight years, and I'm still choking on the aftertaste.

No, I'm not free. I'm chattel, sold for my grandfather's ambitions the moment he found out my parents were having a girl. My father signed off on the deal as soon as he heard how much the Maceo family was worth. That's what matters to him. His own greed. Certainly not his daughter.

I huff at the reminder, casting a longing glance toward the window. How many times have I wished to climb out of it and disappear into the night? Too many to count.

Unfortunately for me, there is no disappearing when you're a Genovese. Not if you want to survive, anyway. Not in this city, and not right now.

Tommaso Genovese dreams of being *Capo dei capi*, of seeing the Genovese family lead the Chicago outfit instead of the Valentinos, and he's dragged the family to the brink of war to make it happen.

He's using Rafael Valentino's own people against him, and Rafael doesn't have a clue. His lawyer, Diego Butera, is working for my grandfather. So is Diego's sister and one of Rafael's enforcers, Carmine. If my grandfather succeeds, he'll topple Rafael from his throne. If he fails, the Valentino brothers will declare war.

Is it any wonder I can't sleep? If Rafael Valentino falls, my life of servitude begins. And if he doesn't...well, God only knows what hell awaits my family then.

No matter the outcome, I lose.

I'm trapped like a rat in a cage, and the walls are closing in on me.

Welcome to your future, principessa. Now, smile and pretend you're having the time of your life.

"*Dio*," I mutter, my stomach churning. My skin grows hot as my throat threatens to close on me. I tug at the neck of my chemise and robe, but it doesn't help. I can't breathe.

I quickly shove my feet into a pair of slippers and throw open the door to my room. The nightlight in the hallway illuminates my path as I race down the hall, tripping over my own feet in my haste to get outside where I can breathe.

The city is every bit as much a prison as this mansion, but at least out there, I can look up at the sky and dream. I still have those, even though everyone says they're impossible. To hell with everyone. They can have my dreams when they pry them out of my cold, dead fingers.

I fly down the stairs, my hand barely touching the banister railing the whole way down. The house is eerily quiet. Either my grandfather has Battista and his goons out scaring the neighborhood children, or they're too busy playing poker in the back to realize that I'm on the move.

Either way, I'm able to slip outside without an escort. I close the door behind me, dragging in a deep lungful of air. The familiar scent of chocolate from the Blommer Chocolate Factory mingles with the earthy notes of the river. Another scent overrides the others. Cologne.

Marcello.

My mood instantly lifts.

I push away from the door, slipping down the path leading around the side of the house toward the garage.

"I thought you were in New York until next week," I say, wrapping my arms around myself as I step through the gates, smiling.

"*Merda.*"

My smile slides from my face as two men I've seen only from a distance turn in my direction, grim-faced and steely-eyed. Domani Brambilla and Coda Passero. Rafael Valentino's men. One of my grandfather's goons hangs between them, his body limp and lifeless.

He isn't the only one. A heap of bodies is already piled in front of the garage doors. Even in the dim light, the blood soaking through their clothing and drying on their faces presents a macabre picture. They're all dead. Every last one of them, Battista amongst them.

And if he's here...then my grandfather is dead too. He never goes anywhere without Battista.

Tommaso Genovese gambled, and he lost.

He lost everything.

The realization comes slowly to a mind numb with shock.

War isn't coming. It's already here.

I should run or scream. I *know* this, and yet, like an idiot, I do neither.

"Is he dead?" I ask.

Coda looks at Domani, who looks at me.

"My grandfather," I clarify.

Domani hesitates and then nods.

"Okay." I'm not sure what else to say. I feel no sorrow, no grief. I feel nothing. My grandfather is dead, and I feel nothing.

What's wrong with me?

I take a step backward, intending to go back inside and do…what? I don't get the chance to find out. I bump into a brick wall that wasn't there a minute ago. One with arms and hands.

Mattia Agostino, Rafael Valentino's consigliere.

"I'm sorry," he says.

For what? I want to ask, but I don't get to do that either. He clamps one hand over my mouth, lifting me off my feet with the other.

My heart gives a jarring thud, jolting my entire system. Then and only then does my mind finally snap into action. The fog lifts as pure terror sweeps in. I fight.

I fight like hell.

And I lose.

Chapter One

CALLANDRIA

I blink my eyes, slowly coming awake. My head swims, making my stomach roil dangerously. I feel like I've been sleeping for years and not well. I groan, trying to remember…anything. But everything is a giant black void.

What happened?

I shift my gaze carefully around the room, taking in my surroundings. Unfamiliar dark red walls and elegant black furniture greet me. A triptych depicting the Chicago skyline dominates the far wall. It's beautiful, but I've never seen it before now. Black and red curtains hang closed over a bank of windows to the right, with a small table and chairs set up in front of them.

Where am I? How did I get here?

I search my mind but find only that damning void again. I don't remember how I got here. Or where *here* even is.

I flatten my hands against the silk sheets to push myself upright. Metal clicks, halting the sluggish movement.

What?

I flip back the plush duvet cover surrounding me, my eyes locking on the padded restraint surrounding my left wrist. A length of chain runs from the metal clip to a hook above the bed.

No. Oh, no.

I already know what I'll find, but I check the right wrist anyway. A matching restraint surrounds it.

I'm chained to the bed.

Fear shoots through my system, clearing some of the cobwebs from my mind. Memory returns, first in a trickle and then in a flood.

My reckless decision to run outside without an escort in the middle of the night.

The pile of bodies outside of the garage—all men I knew, all dead.

Domani Brambilla and Coda Passero, two of Rafe Valentino's enforcers.

Utter terror as a hand clamped down over my mouth from behind.

Fighting for my life as my captor dragged me toward an SUV outside the gates.

And then blessed darkness.

Maybe not so blessed, you fool. You've been kidnapped and chained to a bed. Nothing good has ever happened to a woman chained to a bed.

"Does he know about this?" a man rumbles from the other side of the door, anger seething in his dark tone. His deep voice is familiar. I've heard it somewhere before, but I don't know where or when. Tonight, possibly, though I don't think so. He doesn't sound like Coda, Domani, or Mattia.

"No. Given the circumstances, I thought it best to give him some time."

Another bolt of fear lances through me at the sound of the second man's voice. I've definitely heard it before. Right before I passed out.

Or did he drug me?

I don't remember.

But I remember him. *Mattia Agostino*, the Devil's right hand. If someone dies under order of *La Cosa Nostra* in this city, his boss gave the order. He's ruled over the city with an iron fist since he rose to power. He's ruthless and brutally efficient.

I think I'm going to live long enough to find out just how ruthless and brutal he can be. If I'm here, it's not by chance. His men took me for a reason.

"I should kill you and Domani for bringing her here," the first man growls to Mattia.

"We couldn't take her to him," Mattia says. "Think about it, Luca. Tommaso is dead, and Rafe left a pile of bodies on Emilio's doorstep. The first place he'll look for his daughter is with him. We're trying to stop a war, not start one."

My breath catches in my throat.

Dead. My grandfather is dead. I knew it, and yet it feels as if I'm learning it all over again. My heart twinges with some emotion, but I have no name for it. It isn't grief. Nor is it sorrow. I know exactly who and what Tommaso Genovese was. A monster.

It's hard to grieve what you loathe. But I think I feel sadness anyway.

"*Porca troia*," the angry man, Luca Valentino, growls. "Fine. I'll deal with her. But I'm doing it my way."

Deal with me? His way? Do I even want to know what his way is?

No, I quickly decide. *No, I don't.*

Luca may not be as infamous as his notorious brother, but he's still *mafioso*. He's still a Valentino. And my grandfather may have been a monster, but I figure it takes one to know one, right? He hates—*hated* the Valentino family. My whole life, I've heard about the things they've done. The people they've killed. The crimes they've committed.

Rafe may lead the family, but Luca's behind every business deal they've ever made. He's just as ruthless as his brother. When Rafe wants something, Luca makes sure nothing stands in his way.

Dio. I have to get out of here.

I take a breath, trying to calm the way my heart pounds with anxiety. I quickly examine the chains, giving them an experimental tug. The hook over the bed doesn't even budge. It's tightly anchored. But there's enough chain for me to stand up from the bed if I'm careful about it.

Rolling carefully to my side, I wiggle my way to my feet. My head swims. Mattia definitely drugged me. If I ever get my hands on him....

Ugh! I want to punch him in the throat, though I doubt it'd do me any good. You'd think someone would have taught me self-defense, given the life I was born into, but I guess that was too much to ask.

I was just supposed to trust that my bodyguards would protect me. No one ever considered what would happen if they died. No one ever planned for the day my grandfather pulled everyone from their stations for his big move and failed to tell me I was unprotected. No one prepared me for the day I was captured. I don't think my grandfather even considered it a possibility. He was so convinced he'd win that he didn't consider what would happen to anyone else if he lost. I'm not sure he cared enough about me to think about it.

I was a paycheck and an alliance to him, nothing more. He had no affection for me. He protected me because it was expected of him. Because to do anything less would have been to show weakness. One thing Tommaso Genovese was not was weak.

"Domani and I will go fill him in," Mattia says outside the door. "He'll be able to deny involvement without violating the oath."

Dio. I have to get out of here right now.

I test the limits of my restraints, wobbling on my feet. I thought I was trapped like a rat in my bedroom, but I might as well be in a snake's enclosure here. I can't run or hide. I can barely move more than a couple of feet.

Aside from the nightstand, there's nothing within reach. I stretch to open the drawer of the nightstand, cursing under my breath when I come up empty-handed. There's nothing at all in it.

I reach for the lamp, trying not to sob when I realize it's built into the nightstand.

The bulb.

I stretch forward as far as I can, grasping for the top of the lamp. The only way I can reach is to lift my left arm high over my head to give a little slack on the chain on the right arm.

I work quickly to unscrew the bulb, biting my tongue to keep from sobbing in frustration.

The bulb comes loose in my hand.

"What, precisely, are you planning to do with that, Miss Genovese?" Luca Valentino asks from behind me, his gritty voice soft.

The bulb slips from my hand. I watch in horror as it plummets to the hardwood at my feet...and rolls out of reach.

The frustrated sob I've been holding back escapes before I can stop it. Defeat crashes through me like a tidal wave, a tangle of emotions following in its wake.

I spin on Luca, terrified, confused, and angry.

My breath stalls in my throat at the sight of him. I knew he was beautiful—all the Valentino brothers are devilishly handsome—but I'd never seen him in person before. I've only ever seen him on the news. Perhaps that's why his voice is so familiar to me. His dark hair sweeps back from his forehead, tousled as if he's run his fingers through it. Dark brows slash above arresting, deceptively kind dark eyes. The amused smirk on his full lips infuriates me.

His tie hangs loose around his neck, the first two buttons of his dress shirt undone. The sleeves are rolled up to his elbows, showing the thick, corded muscles of his forearms. Even disheveled, he's formidable, a king among men.

And I'm chained to his bed in my nightgown and a robe, completely helpless.

"Come any closer, and I won't need a weapon," I growl anyway. "I'll kill you with my bare hands."

"Ah," he says quietly, his smirk growing as he pushes the door slowly closed.

The quiet click as the latch catches makes me flinch.

"So you heard us outside, I presume."

"You mean heard you saying you were going to deal with me?" I demand, inching closer to the nightstand as if it offers even an ounce of protection. It doesn't. But I'd far rather stand my ground in front of it than beside the luxurious bed. "I swear I won't be easy to *deal with*, Luca Valentino." I glare in fury, refusing to show him just how terrified I am. I'm a *principessa*. If he's going to kill me, I'll die on my feet, screaming defiance.

"No?" His smirk turns mocking, his expression hardening. "You're chained to my bed, *principessa*. Seems easy enough to me."

Oh, I hate him. He's exactly like my grandfather. A monster.

"Does that make you feel powerful?" I snap. "Is that what you enjoy? Taking helpless women against their wills?" I run my gaze up and down him, filling it with as much contempt as I can muster. "I guess the rumors about you are true, after all."

"What rumors?" he growls, his smirk slipping.

I snort instead of answering. He knows what rumors I'm talking about. Everyone in our world whispers about Luca Valentino and the places he frequents. Sex clubs. BDSM playgrounds. Places promising pure hedonistic paradise for men like him. And yet he's never been linked to anyone. Nothing has ever been confirmed. It's always been unsubstantiated rumors. I don't think they're entirely wrong, though. Not if I'm here now.

Mattia Agostino didn't just bring me to him to keep Rafael Valentino's hands clean. I'm not just chained to his bed for the fun of it. He wants something, and he intends to use me to get it. Well, too bad for him because I don't much care to be used.

"The thing about rumors, Miss Genovese," Luca murmurs after a moment, striding deeper into the room. He moves like a lion, graceful and sure. "They're never entirely accurate. Take the ones about you, for instance. Rumor has it that you're never seen without an escort, and yet here you are."

Oh, he's infuriating.

"Yes, here I am. Because I was kidnapped from my own property. I wasn't aware I needed an escort to get a little fresh air on my own property, but I guess your family no longer plays by the rules," I snap.

"You mean the rule your grandfather violated when he kidnapped Rafe's *regina*?" Luca quirks a brow. "Or would that be the one he violated when he tried to have her kidnapped from Rafe's home?"

"I…" I swallow. "I don't know what you're talking about." It's not a lie. I actually don't know what he's talking about. Who did my grandfather kidnap? When?

"I know you don't."

"Your brother killed him." It's not a question. I already know my grandfather is dead. Domani and Coda confirmed it, but I want to hear the truth from this man.

"Yes."

I nod silently, shivering as a chill rips through me. "My father? My b-brother?"

"Alive." Luca pauses. "They'll stay that way so long as they bow to the *Capo dei capi*."

Will they? Marcello, perhaps. He has no interest in being king of kings. But my father? Will he bow? I don't know. Money talks as far as he's concerned. That's all he cares about. Money and what will make him the most of it.

Luca draws to a stop in front of me, tipping his head down to study me. This close, I see the flecks of gold in his mocha eyes. His rich, earthy scent tickles my senses, making my head spin again.

"You drugged me," I accuse, though the words come out breathless and trembling.

"No, Mattia gave you a mild sedative to calm you down. He was worried you were going to hurt yourself." A frown twists at his lips. "You don't remember?"

"I..." For a long, frightening moment, I don't remember. And then a little flash of memory floats to the surface of my mind. "I had a panic attack. In the SUV."

Luca nods. "You couldn't breathe." His gaze flits across my face, searching again. "How often do you have them?"

"That's not your business." Hell will freeze over before I tell this man anything about the attacks that leave me defenseless and gasping for breath. I've had them for years.

He sighs quietly. "Have it your way, then."

"Plan on it," I snap, lifting my chin in a haughty display even though my legs want to collapse beneath me.

That makes him smile for some reason. He's far too beautiful when he smiles, like a lion at rest. And exactly like a lion at rest, he's still capable of inflicting mortal damage with minimal effort.

"Callandria Genovese," he murmurs. "What should I do with you, *principessa*?"

I don't think he's talking to me, but I answer him anyway. "Let me go, Luca. I...I won't tell anyone I was even here. We can pretend it never happened."

"That doesn't work for me, princess." He reaches toward me, and I flinch backward, but there's nowhere for me to go. His fingertips trail down the side of my cheek before gently encircling my throat.

He doesn't squeeze, but he draws me closer, almost as if compelling me with nothing more than the command in his gaze and his hand around my throat. I sway toward him. Closer. Closer.

Until nothing but a tiny sliver of air separates our bodies. I feel the heat of him searing me, feel the way his aura kisses mine every time he draws a breath.

"The rumors about me aren't entirely wrong, princess," he says, turning his head to place his mouth against my ear. "And I find the sight of you chained to my bed far too appealing to give you up that easily."

Shock runs through me, humming like a bowstring pulled taut. I raise my arm, aiming a slap at his smug, arrogant face.

"Ah, ah," he croons, grabbing my hand before it connects. The bastard smiles. He actually smiles at me. "I'm not one of Tommaso's little *coglioni*. You hit me, and you'll be wearing my handprint on your gorgeous ass to remind you who makes the rules here, *principessa*."

"You wouldn't," I hiss, yanking my hand from his grip.

"Try me, *bella*," he growls.

"If you touch me, I'll never give you what you want, Luca Valentino. Never!"

He smiles again, his eyes dark with promise. "Oh, but you will, Callandria. You're going to give me *exactly* what I want because we both know the only thing you want more than you want out of this room is out of this life. And I'm the only one willing to give you the freedom you crave, *principessa*."

He's lying. I know he's lying. And yet...and yet the look in his eyes says he's dead serious. He's offering me an out. A chance at the future my own family denied me.

"Why? What do you want from me?"

He runs his hand down my arm, leaving gooseflesh in his wake. His molten eyes meet mine, his lips curved at the corners. "You haven't already guessed?" he asks, leaning forward to press his full lips to my throat, just beneath my ear. "I want you."

I gasp, shocked even though I shouldn't be. "I'm not for sale, Valentino," I spit.

"No?" His lips slide along my jaw. My stomach clenches even though it shouldn't. My nipples harden even though they shouldn't. "We all have our price, *principessa*. Name yours. Anything you want."

"Let me go."

His breath pelts my throat, warm and intoxicating, when he chuckles. "Anything but that," he murmurs. "I rather like you right here."

"*Lurido bastardo*," I growl, jerking away from him.

He straightens, that damn smirk still in place as his eyes meet mine. "I'll take that as you considering my offer," he says as if I didn't just insult him. "I'm going to shower."

I watch in silent fury as he winks and then turns on his heel and strides across the room, leaving me chained to his bed.

Chapter Two

LUCA

"*Dio*," I growl, wrapping a fist around my aching cock. I lean back against the stone shower wall and close my eyes, envisioning the curvy little beauty I left chained to my bed. Callandria Genovese. My enemy. And the only woman to get my dick hard in longer than I can remember. As soon as Mattia carried her in tonight, my cock took notice of her plump thighs and soft body. Of her long lashes and delicate little nose. Of her sun-kissed olive skin and waist-length hair.

She's even more beautiful when she's awake. There's fire in her and those amber sirens' eyes. She may be in chains, but she's no delicate little prisoner. She's every inch the *principessa*, spitting defiance as if she were born to do it.

I want her, and I intend to have her. Even if I have to play dirty to get her. If that makes me a filthy bastard as she called me, well, I've been called worse. Hell, I've *been* worse. Rafe's hands aren't the only ones in this family stained with blood. He didn't claw his way to the top alone. Rafe, Gabriel, and I climbed a pile of bodies together. It isn't what he wanted for Gabriel or me, but we made our choice a long time ago. The only hands in this family not stained in blood are Nico's.

Rafe traded his future for Nico's freedom a long time ago. I traded mine to keep my brothers alive. And Gabriel, well, Gabe traded his to keep the three of us together. We'd already lost Nico when he walked away from this way of life. Gabe wasn't going to lose another brother, he said.

We're the fucking three musketeers. One for all. All headed straight to hell.

If I'm damned, I intend to claim Callandria before I take my place in hell. I want her desperate for me. I want her choking on my cock, pleading for it, willing to do anything for one more taste of it. I'm going to own her, body and soul.

Please, Luca, please. Give it to me.

I work my fist up and down my shaft, grunting as I imagine her spread out below me, her amber eyes liquid pools of desire, her body drenched in sweat. She arches and writhes, my name breaking from her plump lips as she pleads for me to fuck her harder.

I want it. Please, Luca. Harder.

"Fuck," I snarl, grasping for the shower wall as my balls draw up and cum shoots up my shaft. My legs threaten to buckle as my seed splashes against the shower floor before being swept down the drain. I suck air into my lungs, working out every last ounce of pleasure before I release my cock and slump against the wall.

How long has it been since I got myself off?

Merda. I can't even remember. Too goddamn long, I know that much.

"Fuck," I mutter, dragging myself beneath the hot water to clean up.

Callandria was only half right about those rumors. There was a time I frequented sex clubs. Ten years ago, I thought I could find what I was looking for inside, so I'd go and watch all manner of kink play out in front of me. I never found what I was looking for within. I never participated. Eventually, I stopped going altogether. There wasn't a fucking point when I always left more restless and dissatisfied than when I arrived.

If I'm going to die, it won't be with my pants around my ankles during some quick fuck in a club. And the possibility of having a knife slipped between my ribs by some chick paid off by one of our enemies wasn't a risk worth taking. Trust is hard to come by in this world. These motherfuckers will hug you with one hand and plunge the knife into your back with the other.

Tommaso Genovese certainly did.

"The shady, honorless motherfucker," I growl to myself, scrubbing shampoo into my hair as if that'll wash out the last month of my life. Genovese deserved death for everything he's done to our family. He had his own people killed to pin their deaths on us. He put a rat in Rafe's home, tried to force Rafe's *regina* to spy on him by holding her life over her head, and then kidnapped her when she refused to do his dirty work for him.

The old bastard's death presents a problem, though. If Emilio decides to seek revenge, he may very well drag everyone into an all-out war. The streets will run red with the blood of *La Cosa Nostra*. No one can afford that. The Valentino family may be strong, but none of us have the numbers we once did. A war will break us.

I don't just want the curvy *principessa* in my bed. I *need* her in my bed. It's the only way to stop what's coming and keep us all from ruin. I just need to convince Callandria that she wants what I'm offering. By the time she realizes I'll never let her go…well, we'll cross that hurdle when we come to it.

Despite what she thinks, I'm not a monster. I won't take her against her will. Her body is her own. But I never said I wouldn't blackmail her into seeing things my way. If her father thinks she's sharing my bed, whatever plans he had for her go up in smoke. Any alliance he thought to forge by dangling her as bait will disappear. He'll be furious. But not even their strongest allies would dare come between a Valentino and his *regina*, not after tonight.

Her own grandfather sealed her fate the minute he made a play for Rafe's queen. I don't have to force her to fuck me. I just have to wait her out. I'll keep her here as long as I have to keep her to convince her to give herself to me. She may think she can resist me, but she's wrong.

My phone rings, vibrating across the countertop. I dip my head under the water to rinse the soap out of it, turn the water off, and step from the shower to grab a towel. Steam swirls around me, fogging up the bathroom.

"*Merda*," I mutter under my breath when Rafe's name flashes across the display. Whatever he has to say, I'm almost positive I don't want to hear it, but I swipe to answer anyway.

"You have Callandria Genovese chained to your bed?" he growls. "What the fuck are you and Mattia thinking?"

"You're the one who decided to deliver a pile of bodies to Emilio's doorstep," I remind him. "Mattia couldn't just leave her there after she spotted them."

"So you *chained her to your bed*?" he growls, his voice deadly quiet. Rafe doesn't yell. He rarely ever raises his voice. When you're the king, you don't have to shout to be heard. People listen even if you fucking whisper. "*Dio*,

Luca. Think! She's a *principessa*, not some *zoccola* you found in a club!"

"Watch your mouth when you're speaking about the mother of my future heir," I warn, my hand tightening around the phone.

"*Cazzo*!" Rafe swears. "What are you doing, Luca?"

"Stopping a fucking war," I growl, scrubbing the towel through my hair. "The one thing Emilio cares about is money. If Callandria is carrying an heir to the Valentino fortune, he'll fall in line. He wouldn't dare start a war if the Genovese family stands to lose a piece of the Valentino fortune. And if he stands down, the families aligned with his will too."

"*Cristo*."

"You know I'm right," I snap. "So why don't you get off my dick and let me do what I need to do to protect this family?"

"Watch your tone, brother."

"Fuck off, Rafe." I may bend a knee in public, but I'll be damned if I do it behind closed doors. I bow to no one, not even Rafe.

"Are you sure about this?" he asks. "You'll be tied to the Genovese family permanently."

"I'm aware." One way or another, this ends with my ring on Callandria's finger. Rafe knows it as well as I do. Emilio Genovese will demand it to secure his grip on the Valentino fortune. I'm just hoping Callandria doesn't figure out that part until she's already pregnant with my kid.

It's a dick move, but I never said I was a good guy. I'll do whatever I have to do to protect my family and claim my queen. And make no mistakes about it, but she will be mine. I refuse to accept anything less.

"You're going to let her go once she's pregnant?" Rafe asks.

My silence speaks for me.

He rattles off a string of curses in Italian, none of them complimentary. And then he laughs abruptly, a sound so rarely used it startles me. "*Manfakulo*, Luca. I hope you know what you're doing. I'm too goddamn old to handle Amalia and your shit too."

"I've got my shit under control," I mutter, tossing my towel toward the hamper. Moving pieces around until we get what we want is what I do. It's kept us alive this long. It'll keep us alive this time too. "How is Amalia, by the way?"

"Sleeping, which is precisely what I'm going to do. I have a feeling I'll be up to my ears in bullshit tomorrow." His heavy sigh sends static down the line. "Unchain her from the goddamn bed, Luca. She's a *principessa*. I'd like to at least have a clear conscience when I violate my oath tomorrow."

"Already planned on it. I'm just letting her cool off. She tried to slap me."

"Do you blame her?" Rafe asks, amusement in his tone. *Dio*. He's in a good mood for a man who just had to rescue his *regina* and kill the head of the Genovese family. Rafe is rarely in a joking mood. When his twin, Nico left the family, he took the softer side of Rafe with him.

He's been slowly losing himself ever since. It's not hard to do when you're chained to an empire you never wanted, and the enemies wait just outside the gates. Gabriel and I have been trying for years to pull him back from the brink with little success. But something clearly dragged him back from the ledge.

It's Amalia. She's bringing him back to life.

For the first time in my life, I feel something I've never felt for Rafe. *Envy*. Not for Amalia. I have no interest in her. But I want to know what peace feels like. So bad I can taste it.

"No," I murmur. "I don't blame her."

By the time I make it back to the bedroom, Callandria is curled up in a tiny ball on top of the bed, sleeping. She looks peaceful in repose, not at all like the fiery woman who called me a filthy bastard.

She's still too beautiful for words. I'm not surprised Tommaso kept her so closely guarded. Contrary to what she believes, we don't make a habit of targeting women. They've always been safe under Rafe's rule. He watched our mother die in the streets. He said he'd be damned if it happened to another woman on his watch. Anyone who targets a woman dies bloody. Tommaso changed that.

I guess he thought if he was willing to violate the rule, others would be too. He may have been a bastard, but he was no fool. Callandria is his only granddaughter. That makes her infinitely valuable. Her angelic looks and soft, ripe body only sweeten the prize she presents. He wouldn't have wanted her falling into the wrong hands.

Too bad for him because she's in mine now. Hell will freeze over before I give her up willingly.

"*Cristo*," I growl to myself. "Get it together." She's supposed to be a means to an end, nothing more. And yet it sure as hell doesn't feel that way. This isn't just about the war, and I damn well know it. Something about *her* has long dormant instincts shaking off their hibernation and rising to their feet. I want her in my bed because I'll be damned if she's in any other.

I have no name for the hot flare of possession. No experience with the burning jealousy. But I feel them when I look at her anyway. She's chained to my bed, under my control, and I still want to destroy any motherfucker who even thinks he has a claim on her. What the fuck do you call that?

Idiocy, Luca. You call it idiocy.

I stomp toward the bed and carefully unhook her right wrist from the restraint. She mumbles incoherently when I lift her arm to inspect it for any marks and then sighs softly.

I repeat the process with the left, relieved to see no marks or bruises from the restraints. She grumbles this time, her brows furrowing.

I fully intend to leave her in peace. At least, I tell myself I do. But I find myself slipping into the bed beside her anyway. Just for a minute.

As soon as I stretch out, she snuggles up against me, pressing her tiny feet up against my calves. I groan, my dick stirring to life as she burrows into me as if I've held her this way a thousand times.

Jesus Christ. She's killing me here.

And I'm going to let her do it.

I don't sleep. I watch over her until the sun lights the horizon and then carefully slip from the bed. I briefly contemplate leaving her unrestrained and then remember her trying to unscrew the light bulb to use as a weapon.

She's liable to hurt herself trying to stab me with whatever random shit she manages to turn into a shiv. I won't allow that. So I regretfully slip the restraints back onto her wrists. I'll remove them once we have a chance to set some ground rules.

I barely manage to get them in place before her amber eyes pop open, settling on me. She blinks once before confusion turns to suspicion.

"What are you doing?" she demands, her voice low and throaty from sleep. She's tousled, a tiny crease across her cheek. "Why are you half naked?"

"Just got up," I say. It's not technically a lie. "I thought you might need to use the restroom." That part is entirely made up. I hoped she'd sleep a little longer so I could catch a few hours.

Her suspicious gaze flits across my face, searching for any hint that I'm bullshitting her. Clearly, my little *principessa* doesn't trust easily, either. She has a survivor's instinct. In this world, it's necessary. Kill or be killed. Doesn't it always come down to one or the other?

Not for her. Never for her.

"I can come back later...."

"No!" She sits up quickly, her tangled hair tumbling down her back. Heat climbs into her cheeks, staining them a dusty pink. "Um, I'll go now."

I jerk my chin in a nod and set to work undoing the restraints I just replaced around her delicate wrists. "Did you sleep well?"

"Does anyone sleep well chained to a bed?" She eyes me balefully.

"I wouldn't know. I've never been in your shoes."

"Want to trade places? I'll play the captor. You can be the helpless hostage," she retorts, sarcasm heavy in her voice. "I'll even let you wear my chains."

A ghost of a smile dances at my lips. "Is this your way of telling me you want to tie me to the bed, *bella*?"

"Only if I can set it on fire once you're in it," she says, batting her lashes at me.

I chuckle, unoffended. Her honesty is refreshing. No one else would even dare speak to me in such a way. Even our enemies watch their mouths when they speak to us. Not Callandria. She doesn't give a flying fuck if I'm a Valentino or the Pope. To her, I'm just the asshole keeping her against her will.

"Go to the bathroom before you get yourself in trouble, Callandria," I say, releasing her from her bonds.

She pulls her hands toward her body, rubbing her wrists as if they hurt. I frown at the sight. Perhaps I missed some bruise or mark?

"How long do you plan to keep me chained like a dog, Luca?" she asks, climbing to her feet.

"That depends."

"On what?"

"Go to the bathroom, *principessa*, and then we'll talk."

She stares up at me for a moment, her lips pursed, and then she huffs. "*Non rompermi le scatole,* Luca Valentino.*" Don't break my boxes, Luca Valentino.* Don't get on my nerves. She sails past me, muttering under her breath.

I grab her arm gently, dragging her back against my chest. "You don't want me to get on your nerves, princess?" I growl in her ear. "Then stop fucking with me. Because every time you open that smart mouth, I want to fuck it."

A soft gasp escapes her lips, full of shock. But seething just below the surface, I hear what she desperately tries to hide. Curiosity. Desire. She's attracted to me. The thought of sucking me off turns her on as much as it pisses her off.

I press my face to her neck, raking my teeth across the sensitive skin beneath her ear. Her pulse hammers there, pounding like a war drum. "Sooner or later, you're going to give in and give us both what we want, *bella*."

"N-no, I'm not."

"Liar," I whisper, nipping her throat before I release her.

She doesn't deny it again. We both know she can't. She wants me. It's only a matter of time until she caves.

"Don't bother trying the bathroom window, *bella*. It doesn't open."

Chapter Three

CALLANDRIA

Everyone has it wrong. Rafael Valentino isn't the devil. Luca is.

I pace around the luxurious bathroom, muttering under my breath like a crazy person as I make the same circuit across the stone tile. I've already used the bathroom, checked the window, and scoured the shelves for a weapon. There isn't anything of use. There isn't even a bottle of cologne I can spray in his gorgeous eyes to blind him.

I'm in no hurry to return to captivity. I even took a quick shower and stole a toothbrush from beneath the sink to delay the inevitable. My heart still races. I *still* feel his lips against my skin, sending shockwaves through my body.

Dio. No one has ever spoken to me the way he does or touched me as if I belong to them. It infuriates me and makes my blood run hot at the exact same time.

Luca Valentino is dangerous. Not to my family. Not because he's *mafioso*. Not because he has blood on his hands. But to *me*.

I like the feel of his hands on my body and the possessive edge to his kisses a little too much. It's madness. Complete insanity. I don't even like him. Yet he touches me and some tiny part of me craves more.

His sharp rap against the bathroom door rattles my nerves. I jump, my heart thudding against the walls of my ribcage.

"I brought you something to wear," he says. "Would you like me to bring it in to you?"

The hint of amusement in his tone sends me scurrying across the bathroom. I quickly unlock the door, thrusting an arm out through a small crack to take whatever he brought before he tries to come in.

He passes me a stack of neatly folded clothes.

"Stop stalling, *bella*. I'm not going anywhere," he murmurs, gently grabbing my wrist before I can pull my arm back. Electricity crackles where his skin meets mine. "If I have to come in there after you, I'll only *get on your nerves* again. And you know how much I like that smart fucking mouth."

Oh! I hope he chokes on his own wicked tongue!

I yank my arm back and slam the door in his face.

"Three minutes, Callandria, and then I'm coming in even if I have to break the door down."

I don't have to ask to know he's serious. He's crazy enough to do it. I quickly strip out of my silk robe and nightgown and throw on the t-shirt and sweats he brought me. I'm a curvy girl, a size twenty, but his clothes swallow me. I tie the shirt up around my waist to make it fit better and then roll the sweats up, mourning the fact that I have no clean panties and no bra. I could desperately use both right about now.

Once I'm finished, I comb my fingers through my hair to tame it, and then lurk in front of the bathroom door, counting down the seconds. I don't have a watch, but I keep time in my head, refusing to emerge a single second before required. It's childish, but I'm not feeling particularly rational at the moment.

My whole world is eroding beneath my feet. I've been taught my whole life that the man outside this room is the enemy. Yet he's offering me the one thing my own family never did: the chance to forge my own destiny. It's too good to be true, yet part of me desperately wants it to be true anyway. I *want* to believe him. That terrifies me, almost as much as the realization that I'm attracted to him.

He could destroy me. It's what he does. Destroys things. Dismantles them. Picks them apart until they have no choice but to be swallowed up by the Valentino empire. If his family is too big to fail, it's not because they build. It's because *he* consumes.

I don't want to be the next item on his agenda. The next project to cross from his to-do list. But I have a feeling that's precisely why I'm here. I'm the tool in whatever harsh lesson he's preparing to teach my family.

I count down to zero and reluctantly push open the bathroom door.

Luca's standing on the other side, reclining against the wall with his eyes closed. He's wearing a shirt this time, all those acres of muscles and olive skin covered. Thank God.

Even relaxed, he's a king among men. This man wasn't made to bow. There's an energy to him, a confidence that only the most powerful Made men possess. It's as if authority hangs in the air around them, stamping them with the cold brand of *Omertà*.

He cracks one eye open, focusing on me. "You didn't waste any time."

"You said I had three minutes."

He smiles, pushing away from the wall. "So I did. Are you hungry, *bella*?"

"Callandria."

"Hmm?"

"My name is Callandria, not *bella*. Not *principessa*. Callandria," I state firmly.

His smile grows. "Are you hungry, Callandria?"

"No," I lie.

He shakes his head, his smile slipping. "Liar. Be angry with me all you want, but don't starve yourself out of spite. Despite what you think, I do care that you're comfortable here."

"Is that what you tell everyone you chain to your bed?"

"Considering that you're the first person I've ever had chained to the bed, I suppose so." He shrugs, crossing to a table set up in front of the floor-to-ceiling windows. "Come. Sit. Breakfast will be up in a moment."

I stare after him, full of doubt. "You aren't going to chain me to the table?"

"Didn't plan on it." He glances over his shoulder at me, amusement in his gaze. "Unless you have a thing for the chains, in which case, I might be persuaded to change my mind."

"Ugh," I growl in disgust, stomping across the room to the table. I toss a scornful look his way before throwing myself down into a chair. "Happy now?"

"Never," he says softly.

I glance up, caught off guard by the serious note in his voice, only to find him tapping out a text on his phone. I watch him for a moment, trying to make sense of him. He's two entirely different people, I think, and I don't know which is the real him. The ruthless mob boss who refuses to let me go, or the wanton, almost playful man who lets me get away with talking to him in a way my own father would never permit?

"We're done with the chains."

I blink, caught off guard all over again.

"You'll have free reign of the house," he says, still tapping away on his phone. "The only thing you can't do is leave or contact the outside world."

"Let me guess. All I have to do is agree to sleep with you," I say, venom in my voice.

He looks up from his phone, his arresting gaze settling on me. "No, *bella*. All you have to do is agree to play by the rules."

"What rules would those be?"

"No going outside, no trying to leave, no trying to contact anyone, and no trying to kill me." He pauses, seemingly considering something. "And you must take care of yourself. No hunger strikes. No endangering yourself. No harming a single hair on your head. That will only piss me off."

"I..." I swallow, the heat in his voice sapping the moisture from my mouth. "Why do you care?" I rasp. "Why am I here? What do you want from me?"

"I want you, Callandria." He settles into the chair across from me, his legs stretched out, one arm resting on his stomach. He's an indolent king at rest, as beautiful as he is dangerous. "As much as I enjoy seeing you in my clothes, I'll have some things delivered for you today."

"Why?"

"I assumed you prefer clothing that fits."

"You know that's not what I meant, Luca."

He nods once and then opens his mouth as if to respond. A knock on the bedroom door silences him. "Come," he growls, flicking his gaze in that direction.

A moment later, the heavy wooden door slides open. An older man with silver hair and age spots pushes a breakfast cart into the room. Laugh lines crinkle the corners of his cinnamon eyes.

His gaze drifts over the chains still attached to the bed as he pushes the cart through the room, but he doesn't comment. He just smiles at me, his expression far warmer than my grandfather's ever was.

"This is Ricardo, *bella*. Ricardo, Callandria Genovese," Luca says, introducing us. "Ricardo has worked for my family since I was a little boy."

I can't imagine Luca Valentino was ever a little boy. He's far too much man for me to envision it.

"Good morning, Miss Genovese."

"Hi," I mumble, not counting on him to help get me out of here. If he's worked for the Valentino family for that long, he's loyal. Luca could murder me in front of him, and he probably wouldn't bat a lash. My grandfather's long-time staff certainly wouldn't. God only knows the secrets they hold.

Ricardo pulls the cart right up to the table before he begins unloading it. As soon as the lid comes off the heaping plate he sets in front of me, the aroma of bacon and eggs wafts toward me.

My mouth waters, and my stomach growls. I press a hand to it, my cheeks flushing.

Ricardo hears it and chuckles. "Cooked it all myself," he says, winking at me. "Best bacon you'll ever eat."

"He's not lying. Eat, *bella*," Luca says gently.

Part of me wants to refuse simply to be difficult, but I can't be rude to an elderly man, even if he does work for Luca. Besides, I'm starving.

I gingerly tear a piece of bacon in two and pop part of it into my mouth. My eyes threaten to roll back into my head as the maple melts on my tongue. Luca watches me with dark, hooded eyes, his attention solely focused on me as I chew. He shifts in his seat, leaning forward.

"Thank you, Ricardo," he mutters, his voice rough. His eyes never leave me as I tear into the other half of the bacon. "I'll have someone handle cleaning up our mess when we're finished eating. Maria is probably waiting for you over at the rest home. You should get over there before she starts raising hell."

"Stop trying to charm my wife away from me," Ricardo says. "You know she's past her hell-raising days, and I'm too old for you to have her thinking any different."

Luca chuckles quietly.

There's an easy familiarity between them that I'm not prepared for, a level of affection that throws me off-balance. Luca doesn't speak to Ricardo as if he's beneath him or simply an employee, but as if he's an old friend. And Ricardo doesn't speak to Luca as if he's feared or has to carefully watch what he says, but as if he's free to say what he wants. It's...unexpected.

"Have a good day, Miss Genovese." Ricardo tips an imaginary hat at me and then grasps the handles of his pushcart and begins his slow trek back across the bedroom.

I grab my linen napkin from the table to wipe my mouth. "Thank you, Ricardo," I call, my mind spinning. I watch in contemplative silence as he exits the room, pulling the door closed behind him. When I turn back to the table, Luca's staring at me. "His wife is in a nursing home?"

"You eat. I'll talk," he says.

I roll my eyes but pick up my fork and scoop up a bite of eggs. They're just as good as the bacon, even better, perhaps.

"Dementia," he says quietly. "They have a house on the property here, but her condition eventually became too much for him to manage alone. I helped him place her in a private facility where she has the best care possible. He should be retired, but he's a stubborn old man. He cooks breakfast and does odd jobs around the house. It makes him feel like he's earning his keep and contributing to her care."

"That's...really sweet."

"Surprised?" He arches a brow, smirking at me.

"Yes," I say honestly. Generosity isn't something I've seen much of in my life. My grandfather certainly wouldn't have done the same for anyone in his employ. Neither would my father. He isn't a monster like my grandfather. He's just...self-centered. The world begins and ends with him and his problems as far as he's concerned. Other people and their problems simply don't exist to him. Unless they're making him money, they fail to register on his radar.

"Your opinion of me is that low, huh?" Luca says, his smirk slipping.

"All I know about you is what I've been told. And what I've seen since I've been here." I spear another bite of egg. "Chaining me to the bed all night didn't win you any favors."

"You weren't chained all night, *bella*."

I glance up at him.

"You slept in my arms all night," he says. "You slept peacefully." A teasing smile dances at his lips. "You like to cuddle."

"I do not."

"You do." His dark gaze slides across my face, hot and hungry. "I never knew it could be so...stimulating."

I drop my fork with a clatter, placing my hands on the table to push myself to my feet.

"Forgive me, *principessa*," he says with a sharp shake of his head. "I'm not trying to get on your nerves. You seem to bring it out of me."

"So it's my fault you can't have a single conversation without being a jerk?"

"No. It's your fault I can't think because my cock is so hard it hurts," he growls. "No one speaks to me the way you do. The more you fight me, the harder it makes me. The longer I look at you, the more I ache to taste you. You're driving me fucking crazy, *piccolina*."

"What do you want from me?" I cry, my stomach clenching at the look in his eyes, as if he's never been more serious in his life. He means every word. I may be here for a reason, but he wants me for exactly the reasons he just said. And that scares me and doesn't scare me nearly enough at the same time.

I expect him to give me the same non-answers he's been giving me, but he doesn't. He surprises me this time. He gives me the truth. At least, some version of it. "I want you to help me stop a war, Callandria," he says, sitting back in his chair. "You grandfather started something that may very well destroy us all. I need you to help me stop it."

My stomach trembles as the pieces begin to connect in my mind. I don't need him to spell it out for me. I know exactly what he's asking of me. And yet...and yet I want to hear him say it anyway. "Tell me," I say.

"I want you to give me an heir." He holds my gaze, unflinching. "In exchange, you'll have your freedom. Whatever marriage contract your grandfather sold you into disappears. You'll have the opportunity to pursue college, a career, whatever you choose to do. All you have to do is say yes."

He makes it sound so simple, but we both know things are never simple in this world. All I have to do is forsake my family and turn my back on everything I was ever taught. All I have to do is crawl into bed with the brother of the man who killed my grandfather, with my family's sworn enemy. If there's a war brewing, I'm supposed to be on the opposite side. They left a pile of bodies on our doorstep—men I've known my entire life.

"Tommaso Genovese was the only one who wanted a war," Luca says quietly. "Rafe would never have raised a hand against him had he not started this entire thing. If your father chooses to retaliate, it will be a blood bath."

I only know what Marcello has shared with me and what tidbits I've picked up from listening when I shouldn't have been, but I've put together enough to know Luca probably isn't wrong about that. Eye for eye, tooth for tooth, and burn for burn. It's a dangerous way to live, but it's the only way these men know. Unless they have a reason to stop, they never will.

A Genovese-Valentino heir would be a reason. It would be a massively big reason.

"What happens if I don't agree?"

"You stay until I convince you."

"What happens, Luca?"

His jaw clenches, his eyes turning hard. "Your father knows exactly where you are and whose bed you're sleeping in," he states, his voice clipped. He reaches into his pocket and pulls out his phone, doing something on the screen. His eyes meet mine over the top of it before he slowly turns it around. "And he believes you're here by choice."

I stare at the photo on the screen in shock. It's the two of us in his bed. I'm snuggled up against him, my arm thrown over his stomach, my head resting peacefully on his chest. He's holding my ass in one hand, a look of pure possession on his face as he stares into the camera. I don't look like a prisoner. He doesn't look like my captor. We don't look like enemies. We look indecently, scandalously intimate.

Out of the corner of my eye, I spot my fork. I grab it, lunging across the table for him as hurt and anger crash together like cymbals in my chest. I believed him. I actually believed him when he said he wasn't going to force me.

He drops his phone, grabbing me around the waist.

Somehow, he hauls me across the table into his arms. I land on his lap, straddling him with my arms locked together behind my back. He keeps me pinned there embarrassingly easy. He doesn't even break a sweat. The bastard doesn't even work for it. He just subdues me like I'm a toddler in the throes of a tantrum.

His mouth comes down on mine in a hard kiss, his tongue sweeping into my mouth to steal my breath. He takes the tiniest taste of me and then breaks away, breathing hard.

"What did I tell you, *principessa*?" he growls, his lips inches from mine. "I'm not one of your grandfather's little playthings. Lash out at me, and I lash back."

"You're a liar," I seethe.

"No, I never lied."

"You said you wouldn't force me. What do you call this, Luca?" I spit at him, struggling in his arms. "You leave me no choice, and you know it!"

"I leave you the best choice I can leave you, Callandria. Your grandfather put us here. I'm doing what I have to do to ensure you have a family to return to. Would you prefer we murder your father and brother now?" he growls. "Is that the choice you'd prefer we make?"

I flinch, my eyes filling with tears at the thought.

"Because that's the choice I'm left with, *bella*. Either end this fucking war before it can start or leave a trail of bodies behind, starting with the people you love." He presses his forehead to mine. "Whether you give yourself to me is your choice. Your body is yours. I won't take it from you. If I have to make war, then I make war. But I will never take what you don't freely offer. I may be an asshole, but I'm not a goddamn monster."

"Luca."

His lips brush mine in a soft kiss before he stands up suddenly, bringing me with him. "Next time you try to stab me with a fork, make sure you don't miss, *bella*. Otherwise, you'll be walking around with my handprint on that gorgeous ass for days. Finish your breakfast. I have things to do."

He releases me, striding toward the door. I watch him go in silence, too stunned to speak. Not because I hate him but because he might be right. His choice isn't any better than mine. I think it might be infinitely worse.

The door closes behind him with a click.

I collapse into his chair and let the tears fall.

Chapter Four

LUCA

The sound of Callandria's crying slips beneath the door, twisting my stomach into knots.

I made her cry.

Every fucking tear feels like it's eviscerating me.

I wasn't prepared for that. I did what I had to do, but I didn't enjoy it. I don't want her to be a fucking pawn. I don't want her in my bed because she feels like she has no choice.

I want her to feel something for me. I want her all twisted up in knots like I am, unable to keep her mind off of me.

I don't want to be a goddamn monster to her. I want to be the man she can't live without.

Dio.

This isn't how this was supposed to go. I wasn't supposed to feel her rooting her way into my heart. And yet that's precisely what's happening. I'm falling for her. No. That's not true.

I started falling the minute she tried to slap me. I fucking landed sometime in the middle of the night when she was in my arms, defenseless and trusting.

I clench my hands, pressing my forehead to the cool wood, fighting the urge to storm back inside and scoop her into my arms. It's powerful, overwhelmingly so. But I'm not stupid. She'd rip my balls off and feed them to me if I tried to offer her comfort now.

The only thing I'll accomplish by going back in there is cementing her hatred for me.

Fuck Tommaso Genovese and his rabid thirst for power. And fuck Vincent Valentino for saddling us with his goddamn empire.

I push away from the door, unsettled in a way I've never been. Uneasy in a way that's entirely new. I'm used to living with my back against the wall and a sword hanging over my head. But feeling like I've made a mistake? Never.

Alessio Cascieri, my six-foot-six lieutenant, leans against the wall a few paces down the hall, cloaked in shadows. His dark eyes settle on me, as black as the suit encasing his broad shoulders. There's no judgment in them, no recrimination. He watches me placidly, as if I routinely stand rooted outside my bedroom door, listening to Callandria Genovese cry.

"Watch her," I snap at him. "She can go anywhere in the house she wants, but she isn't to step so much as a toe outside."

Cristo. I am the *stronzo* she believes I am. Because I still want her badly enough to keep her here. Even if the threat of war were removed, I'm not so sure I'd be willing to let her go.

She spent one night in my arms, and I want more. I want...forever. However long it takes to win her trust and her heart. That's what I really want from her. Every single piece of her, down to her soul.

"Yep," Alessio says in his usual manner. He doesn't say much. He speaks only when he has something important to say. The rest of the time, he just doesn't fucking bother. People assume it means he's slow. People are wrong. There isn't much Alessio doesn't know. Unlike most of us, he had the chance at a life outside of this world. He took the oath anyway.

"Don't touch her or let anyone else touch her either, Alessio," I growl, heading for the stairs. I still taste her on my lips. Still smell my soap on her skin. Whether she wants my protection or not, she has it. It's a necessity.

"If they do?"

I pause in mid-step, turning back to him. Possessive jealousy rattles through me at the thought of anyone putting their hands on her. I'm still pissed Mattia did. It's irrational, but nothing about the way I feel right now is rational or logical.

"Call me," I say, my voice deadly quiet. "I'll make sure they live long enough to regret it."

I jog down the stairs, my mind still reeling over the little *principessa* in my bed.

Antonio Buratti meets me at the bottom, his expression carved from granite. Like Alessio, his black suit is impeccable. The man probably carries more firepower than the Secret Service, but not a hint of it shows. "Boss called a sit-down," he says.

Great. Rafe is on his bullshit this morning.

"Gabriel?" I ask.

"On the way."

I jerk my head in a nod, already knowing it's going to be a long fucking day. "I'll be ready in five. Have the SUV waiting."

"You're the boss," Antonio says, his expression not changing. He's well aware of who is in my bedroom right now and what Rafe wants to discuss. Like Alessio, he's one of my men, but we all answer to Rafe at the end of the day. Gabriel and I may share a certain amount of power, but Rafe leads the family. His word is law...and as far as they know, I just violated one of his laws. I targeted a *principessa*. I'm holding her against her will. Antonio is worried.

I don't try to ease his mind. We've all got plenty to worry about right now. I'm juggling fire, and I know it. If I drop a torch, we may all go up in flames.

By the time we pull up by the dock at the harbor, Gabriel is already there. He leans against the side of his Harley, skipping pebbles across the water.

He doesn't even glance over his shoulder to see who pulled up. I don't think my youngest brother gives a fuck anymore. He tried for years to keep us together, but this way of life wears on you. By the time he had his accident a few years ago, he wasn't the same kid who spoke the vow.

He's harder. Darker. We rarely see him unless he has no choice. I think he'd walk away from all of it if he could. Hell, which of us wouldn't? None of us wanted this bullshit. We did what we had to do. Just like always.

"You're early," I observe, striding across the dock toward him.

"You're late." He lets another rock fly. It skips three times before sinking, dragged to the bottom to rest alongside decades worth of evidence of *La Cosa Nostra* crimes. *Merda*. Ours aren't the only secrets this harbor keeps. The waters of this city are tainted with the sins of its people.

Gabriel skips another rock and then dusts his hands before glancing over at me. "So you have the Genovese girl," he says.

"You heard."

He jerks his chin in a nod.

"Rafe?"

"Mattia."

"*Dio*. Is nothing secret?" I growl.

"When you have a *principessa* chained to your bed?" Gabe snorts. "Not fucking likely."

"She isn't chained to my bed. Where have you been anyway?"

"Minding the business that pays me." He shrugs. "Rafe told me to stay the fuck out of it and handle the company, so I stayed the fuck out of it and handled the company. Why?"

"You know Nico and Rafe are talking again?"

Gabe's hazel eyes widen. "Since when?"

"Since Nico's girl saw Rafe kill Carmine."

"You're shitting me." Gabe gapes at me. "You aren't shitting me. *Cristo*. And they didn't try to kill each other?"

"Apparently not," I mutter, leaning up against the railing of the dock. "They kissed and made up. Mattia didn't give me a whole lot of detail. All I know is that Rafe and Nico are talking again, and it's looking promising."

"Well, that took long enough," Gabe mutters.

"Nineteen years," I say quietly. They've barely spoken since Nico left home when they were eighteen. I blame our father for that. He wanted an heir, and he got one. He just destroyed his oldest sons to accomplish it. As if seeing our mother gunned down in the street wasn't traumatic enough for the two of them. *Merda*. Is it any wonder we're all fucked up?

Gabriel shakes his head. "What are you doing with the Genovese girl, Luca? I thought we were supposed to be dragging Rafe away from the edge, not pushing him closer toward it."

"That's what I'm trying to do," I mutter, my shoulders tensing.

"By holding her against her will?" Gabe shoots me a look that says he knows I'm full of shit. "We aren't our father, big brother. We aren't Tommaso Genovese. We don't do this shit."

"*Cazzo*," I growl. "Did Rafe call a sit-down, or is this a setup?"

"He called," Gabe says. "I'm just speaking the truth. You know I am."

"I intend to marry her," I mutter, turning to look out at the water. A ship loaded with crates slowly bobs along the water, headed toward Milwaukee. I'm not sure where the confession comes from, but it's true. I want my ring on her finger. Not because Emilio will demand it but because I want it there.

No, principessa. I'm not a monster. I'm just the man you obsessed.

"*Cristo*. Does Emilio know?"

"He will soon enough."

"Does she know?"

I shrug noncommittally.

Gabe is silent for a moment and then barks laughter. "Fucking hell. First, Rafe starts thinking with his dick, and now you are."

"You have no idea what you're talking about."

"No? You think Emilio will just hand her over? Marcello?" Gabe laughs again, a hard, mocking edge to the sound. "You aren't that stupid, Luca. Emilio is a leech, but Marcello will try to rip your throat out if he gets a chance. He and Callandria are tight."

"Which is precisely why they think she left of her own free will."

"Jesus Christ," Gabe mutters. "You've lost your goddamn mind."

I spin to face him, only to see Rafe's Bentayga pulling up beside my SUV. I snap my mouth closed, waiting silently for our older brother to join us before we hash this shit out. If I'm going to have to argue my case again, I'd rather do it with both of them at once. This will be the last time I do it.

Explaining my decisions isn't something I make a habit of doing. They're the only two who get the courtesy. Anyone else can fuck off as far as I'm concerned. I'm not Rafe. I don't snap my fingers and expect people to fall in line. But this isn't a democracy, either. Explaining invites questions, questions breed doubt. And doubt is the motherfucker that gets people killed.

I'm trying to make sure as many of us make it out alive as possible. Not just today but every day. That's my job. Making sure we survive.

Gabe glances over at the Bentayga, his eyes hard as he waits for Rafe to emerge from his armored SUV to join us. He grunts when Mattia slips out and heads our way too. Guess he's not thrilled with Mattia's role in any of this shit, either.

Rafe looks nothing like he did when I left him yesterday. The stark hopelessness in his eyes is gone, replaced with a sense of peace I've never seen. Even though his expression is grim, he's settled, happy. It's fucking weird to see from a man who hasn't known peace since he was shot twice when he was an eleven-year-old kid.

"Gabe, Luca," he says. "Thanks for meeting."

I jerk my chin in a nod.

"We live to serve," Gabe says dryly.

Rafe ignores his smart-ass comment. Gabe needles the hell out of him. He's been doing it since our father died and Rafe took over. Gabe belongs in this world about as much as Nico does, but he took the oath. He won't forsake it now. He sits in his ivory tower, running the day-to-day operations of Valentino International.

"Emilio Genovese knows you have his daughter," Rafe says to me, not wasting any time. "He wants a sit-down with you to discuss her return."

"Not happening."

"He isn't buying that she's with you of her own free will."

"Hold the fuck on," Gabriel interrupts. "You knew about this?"

Rafe grimaces, which is answer enough for Gabe.

"You have got to be fucking kidding me," he growls. "You've both lost your minds."

"Watch your mouth, little brother," Rafe snaps. "We're trying to prevent a war."

"Holding the man's daughter hostage is a real great way to accomplish that," Gabe retorts. "As soon as she's free, he'll hit us with everything he has."

"Not if she's carrying Luca's kid."

"Assuming she doesn't dip out before that happens," Gabe says. "Assuming everything goes according to your idiotic plan. Assuming an awful fucking lot."

"He won't strike while she's with Luca," Rafe explains calmly. "He won't risk her."

Huh. So he didn't recruit Gabe to bust my balls. He's arguing my case.

"*Cazzo Madre di Dio*!" Gabe growls, throwing his hands up. "You're both insane."

"They do what they have to do," Mattia says. "You know they do, Gabriel."

Gabriel grunts. "Fine. Then we do what we have to fucking do. And if it makes us no better than Tommaso Genovese, so be it. At least she isn't chained to the bed, right?" he snaps, his jaw clenched tight.

"You untied her?" Rafe asks.

"Always planned on it," I mutter. "Can you stall on the sit-down?"

"How long do you need?"

"How long can you get me?"

"Not long," he mutters. "Given everything that just went down, I can hold him off for a couple of days until cooler heads prevail, but that's it."

"Do it." I hesitate. "I'll get her on the phone with him to help hold him off."

"You sure that's wise?"

"Fuck no," I say, laughing without humor. "But I'll figure it out."

Rafe nods. "Figure it out then. We need to get this shit under control sooner rather than later. Tommaso was found early this morning. But they know who took him out. They know why we left a pile of bodies on Emilio's doorstep too. They also know the *bastardo* had it coming, but Emilio can't be seen as weak if he wants to secure the votes to take Tommaso's place. He either needs to hit back or secure his throne another way."

"An alliance will secure it," I murmur.

Rafe nods his agreement.

Gabe snorts.

"They don't have the numbers to survive a war," Rafe reminds him. "Tommaso was picking off his own people for weeks, and we took out four of his captains and half a dozen of his enforcers last night. We also took out Battista. If Callandria is tied to Luca, Emilio secures the future of the Genovese family. They won't like it, but it's their best choice."

"*Cristo*," Gabe mutters. "It's a hell of a way to secure his place."

He's not wrong. It's ruthless and brutal, little more than a hostile takeover. To secure his place, Emilio Genovese ties himself to the family that murdered his father and nearly destroyed his family. But his family survives. They rebuild. And they do it with Valentino money. It's better than the *figlio di puttana* deserves.

More importantly, it sends a message to anyone else who thinks to try what Tommaso did. Push us, and you'll know what it is to feel the weight of our boots on your neck. It's not a message we intend to have to send more than once. It has to be brutal. It's the only way the lesson sticks.

"Fine," Gabe sighs, giving in to the inevitable. "Do what you have to do."

Chapter Five

CALLANDRIA

By the time I cry myself out, my head throbs faintly. I curl up on the bed and sleep for a while, only to dream of war. The streets run red with blood, and I walk across a pile of bones on my way...somewhere. I don't know where I'm going or who I'm looking for, but I can't find them.

And then I see him.

Luca.

He's laid out in the middle of the street outside my father's house, lifeless and still. Covered in blood. A gun rests beside his hand. The other is outstretched as if reaching for me.

No, Luca. No.

I gasp and rush forward, racing as fast as I can to reach him. Someone grabs me before I can, holding me back.

I scream...and sit bolt upright in the bed, gasping for breath. Shadows overtake the room, darkening the corners. A pile of shopping bags sit just inside the bedroom door. I've been sleeping for hours.

"*Merda*," I whisper, pressing the heels of my hands to my eyes as if that will erase the awful images hovering behind them. It doesn't. I still see him, his face pale. His chest not moving. My own aches in protest, my stomach clenching.

It was just a dream. And yet...it wasn't. It's one possible outcome of whatever decision I make.

Two roads diverged in a mansion....

I drag myself from the bed and stumble to the bathroom to take care of business and splash water on my face. Once that's done, I try the bedroom door. To my surprise, it's unlocked. I poke my head out.

"Miss Genovese."

I jump a foot into the air, whipping my head around to face the giant standing in the shadows across the hall. He blends with the dark wood of the wall, his black suit making him almost invisible. Has he been there all day?

Who am I kidding? Of course he has.

Luca wouldn't leave me here alone, especially after I tried to stab him with a fork this morning.

"Who are you?" I ask, eyeing the giant warily. He's been eating his Wheaties because he's massive. His expression is carved from granite, his eyes dark.

"Alessio Cascieri. Luca asked me to protect you."

"Protect me or babysit me?"

"Protect."

"Then I'd like to go home, please."

A hint of a smile tugs at his lips. "And babysit."

I nod, satisfied with his answer. At least he's honest about his priorities. "And where is Luca?"

"Out."

I know enough to know that's the only explanation I'll be getting from this man. Their vows are inviolable. Even if I tortured him, he wouldn't tell me anything. Luckily for him, I'm not in a torturing people kind of mood. "Can you take me to the kitchen, please? I'd like to find something to eat."

He jerks his head in a nod and steps away from the wall.

"Um, one moment, please." I quickly slip back into the bedroom and close the door, kneeling to rummage through the bags. They're full of clothes. I don't even want to know how Luca knew my size, but nearly everything will fit me except the shirts. They're all too small. It had to have cost him a fortune. I pick out a pair of lacy panties and buttery soft yoga pants and slip them on before grabbing a bra. I strip out of Luca's shirt, put the bra on, and then pull his t-shirt back on over my head, tying it up around my waist again.

"I'm ready," I tell Alessio less than a minute later, stepping back out of the bedroom.

He leads me down the hallway. Unlike my father's house, Luca's isn't built like a museum to wealth. It's timeless and beautiful. Dark wood panels line the walls, with ornately carved banisters and balustrades. Instead of a chandelier, a crystal dome over the staircase floods the foyer with natural light.

We pass through the living room, decorated more for comfort than to impress. A large fireplace and sectional dominate the room, with bookcases lining one wall. Massive doors lead out to a patio and a rolling green lawn.

"Kitchen," Alessio says, standing to the side to let me pass.

I step inside and then stop to stare. The entire kitchen is made from stone, with a cobblestone floor and gorgeous dark wood cabinets. Appliances rest in arched alcoves. Windows look out over the lawn. It's breathtaking, like stepping straight into Tuscany.

"Wow," I whisper. No wonder Ricardo likes to cook breakfast here.

"You like it?" Luca says from behind me.

I spin around to face him, startled by the sound of his voice. He's standing just inside the doorway, watching me intently. He looks exhausted. And alive. The knots in my stomach loosen, the lingering effects of the nightmare falling away. He's not dead in the streets because I made the wrong decision. He's right here. Alive.

"It's beautiful," I whisper, not sure if I'm talking about him or the kitchen.

"Are you hungry, *bella*?"

"Yes."

He steps into the kitchen, close enough I can smell his cologne again. Or maybe it's just him. His scent. I don't know, but my core clenches, heat sweeping through me in a rush. "Would you like me to make you something?"

"You cook?"

"Occasionally."

"Is it edible?"

He smirks at me, holding out a hand. "Come and see, *principessa*."

I stare at his hand for a protracted moment, and then take a breath and place my hand in his. His fingers close around mine, his grip...comforting. He looks at our interlaced fingers for a second and then pulls me deeper into the kitchen.

"You were gone all day," I say as he pulls out a stool at the island for me.

"I had things to attend to."

"What kind of things?" I pry, allowing him to help me up onto the stool. My feet don't touch the ground. I'm not even that short. I'm five-seven. Next to him, I feel small. I should feel unsafe. I should feel endangered. But I don't. I just feel…delicate.

"Things you don't need to know about, *bella*. You don't belong in this world. It's dark and ugly and full of fucked-up, filthy shit that should never touch you," he says near my ear before striding toward the fridge.

I watch him as he searches through it, pulling items out to inspect them. Some make it to a pile on the counter. Others quickly get put back. He works efficiently, completely at ease in the kitchen.

"I was born into this world," I say quietly. "Whether I belong in it or not, I'll never escape it. My family's name will follow me no matter what. If I'm lucky, I'll survive. If I'm not, those dark, ugly, filthy things will touch me. They'll drown me like they do so many of you. That's how it goes, Luca. I'm not free. I'll never be safe. I didn't have to take the vow to be bound by it. When you're female, it hangs over your head without you speaking a word. *That's* what it means to be a *principessa*, Luca. *That's* the weight that sits on my chest."

It's the same one that crushes the air from my lungs and screams at me to flee even though there's nowhere to run. The arm of the law is long. The arm of *La Cosa Nostra* is longer. Even if I fled, my family would find me. They'd drag me back to fulfill the promise they made before I was even out of diapers. Their honor demands it. *Omertà* demands it. Their own greed demands it. I've always been a pawn, moved around a board before I even knew I was a part of the game.

There's nothing this man could tell me that would surprise me, but I need him to tell me anyway. As much as he can, anyway. It's the only way I'll ever be able to trust him. Because I'm done being a pawn. If we're going to forge an alliance to stop a war, I have to be able to trust him.

And right now, I don't. I'm not even sure I trust myself. How can I when my own body betrays me, and my mind lays traps for me even in my sleep?

"*Cazzo*," he growls, turning to face me. His mocha eyes blaze with unholy fire as he paces toward me. "You will be safe, Callandria. I'll rip this city to the fucking ground myself before I let anything happen to you."

My heart thuds against my breastbone in a powerful jolt. He means it. *Dio*. This man really would set this city on fire and watch it burn for me. Why? Why does he care what happens to a Genovese? Just when I think I understand him a little bit, I realize I understand nothing at all.

He circles around the island to me, dragging my chair around to face him. The metal feet screech across the cobblestone floor, but he doesn't seem to notice.

"No one touches you. No one harms you," he snarls, wrapping his hand around my throat to tip my head back. "I'll kill anyone who tries."

"Why?" I whisper, desperate for one straight answer from him. This is more than pride or honor or whatever these men fight about. I feel it radiating from him in waves, but I have no name for it. It's nothing I've ever experienced before. But some part of me cries out in recognition. Some part of me feels the same inexplicable, confusing *something* for him.

"Because you're mine, *piccolina*," he rasps. His mouth slants down on mine, and I find that perhaps I do have a name for what's happening between us, after all. Fate. This man, this moment, all of this.... I think he's my fate. I prayed this moment into existence my whole life. I wanted out so badly, I begged for a miracle.

God answered. He sent me a Valentino to set me free or lead me to ruin. It can only be one or the other. I don't know which path leads to salvation and which leads to damnation. All I know for sure is that with Luca's lips on mine and his hand around my throat, I find a part of myself I've never met before. One desperate to feel this wicked, wanton man everywhere.

Not to forge an alliance. Not to stop a war. But because the thought of not having him all over me is a physical ache, growing stronger by the minute.

I whimper against his lips, silently pleading for relief from the turmoil.

"Fuck," he growls, dragging me out of my chair and into his arms. His hands grip my ass hard, as if he has every right to touch me like no one else ever has.

I should stop him, but I don't want to. Instead, I wrap my legs around his waist, gasping when the hard ridge of his erection settles between my thighs.

"Feel it, *principessa*," he breathes against my lips. "You're responsible for it."

"Luca," I groan. "I...I..." I don't know what I'm trying to say. I don't know what I'm doing. I just know that my body burns like the surface of the sun, and it's not nearly hot enough to satisfy me.

"Work your hips, Callandria. Get nice and acquainted with what belongs to you. You'll be choking on all nine inches soon, *bella*." He bites my lip, dragging it through his teeth as he grinds me against his erection. "You may be a *principessa*, but in my bed, you'll be my little fuck doll, *piccolina*."

"*Bastardo*," I moan without heat, my core clenching at the filthy way he speaks to me.

"Yes, and you fucking love it," he growls, jostling me against him again. His erection grinds against my clit, and I see stars. "I bet your little panties are soaked right now because I'm a bastard. You love me filthy, *bella*. You love fighting me." He presses his lips to my ear. "And you fucking love the thought of belonging to a man who would kill for you, no questions asked."

I want to deny him. I want to call him a liar and say it isn't true, but God help me...I think maybe it is. I don't want to be a pawn. I don't want to be a *principessa* with no choices and no freedom. I want to be the reason someone is willing to risk everything. No, not someone. This man. I want to be the reason *this* man risks everything.

Maybe we aren't so different after all.

"Fucking come, *bella*. Now." He sinks his teeth into my throat, delivering a stinging bite that delivers a pulse straight to my clit. And then he sucks hard, putting his mark on me.

I cry out in bliss, in defiance…I hardly know which I feel. But my body bows to him. And I submit.

The orgasm crashes through me in a powerful wave, knocking my defenses asunder.

He slips beneath them, leaving a brand on my soul.

"I met with my brothers today."

I glance at him, startled. It's the first words he's spoken since he placed a gentle kiss on my forehead and helped me back into my chair half an hour ago. I haven't spoken either. I don't even know where to begin.

"Oh," I say.

"They don't want a war either."

"You think my family does?"

He's silent for a moment as he stirs the sauce. "I think Tommaso left them no choice," he says after a moment. "Your father can't show weakness if he wants to secure the title. If he does nothing to retaliate for Tommaso's murder, he risks losing the vote to someone else. His only other option is to strengthen the family another way, by forging an alliance that dramatically improves their position. If he does that, they may be willing to overlook the fact that he let Tommaso's murder go unpunished, given the untenable position Tommaso put them in."

I turn this information over in my mind, not sure where to fit it. Surprised he gave it to me at all. It's more than I expected.

"A Valentino alliance would improve their position," I state. It's not really a question. Everyone knows the Valentinos are the most powerful family in Chicago. They're also the only family with no recent blood-ties to any of the other families. As it stands, their empire ends with Rafe, Luca, and Gabriel. Any family who manages to hitch themselves to that cart stands to inherit the kingdom, or a massive portion of it, anyway.

"Yes." His clipped tone gives me pause.

"There's something you aren't telling me."

He turns the sauce off, removing it from the heat before slowly turning to face me. "Your father would be aligning himself with the family that virtually destroyed his, *bella*," he says quietly. "It won't be pretty. The others will see it as something akin to a hostile takeover. He'll lose respect, be seen as a mouthpiece for the Valentinos."

I flinch.

"This is what it means to be *mafioso*, *bella*. This is what *Omertà* demands of us," he says quietly. "We do what we must to protect the family, even when we don't like it."

"Is that what you do? Protect your family?"

Luca nods. "The only fucking reason I took the vow was to keep Rafe and Gabriel alive." He chuckles ruefully. "They have not made it easy. Rafe is Rafe. He breathes and has a target on his back. And Gabriel has a hard-on for fast cars and living on the edge."

"You're the reasonable brother?" I ask, doubt heavy in my voice.

He hears it and smiles. "No. That would be Nico, Rafe's twin. The only one smart enough to get the fuck out," he murmurs, a shadow passing through his expression.

"The scientist."

Luca nods.

Marcello told me enough of the story long ago. Vincent Valentino demanded an heir, and Rafe fell on the sword so his twin could have his freedom. It destroyed Rafe and Nico's relationship, though I'm sure why. I opt not to ask. It's not really my business.

But hearing about him now brings something into focus that I hadn't considered before. Luca knows what it's like to lose people to this life. His mother was murdered, and he and his brothers have spent two decades at odds with Nico. He's already experienced the worst this world has to offer.

And despite everything, he's here right now, trying to keep my family from losing anyone they don't have to lose. He doesn't owe it to us. After the machinations and manipulation from my grandfather, most people wouldn't bother. But he's here anyway.

If I can keep that nightmare from coming true, I have to try. His family has lost enough. He's lost enough.

"I'll do it," I blurt.

Luca looks at me unblinking.

"I'll do it," I say again. "I'll help you."

"Why?" he growls.

Because I think I'm falling in love with you.

"Because I don't want to lose anyone," I say instead of speaking that terrifying truth.

Chapter Six

LUCA

Dinner with Callandria is a quiet affair. We're both locked in our own thoughts, wrestling with our own minds. I thought her agreement would satisfy me, yet victory feels hollow and empty.

I want her heart and her trust. Without those, I'm little better than the *bastardo* she called me. *Dio*. I'm tangled in knots for her, and she has no idea.

"Here." I slide my phone across the table to her once we've both finished eating. "You should call your father, *bella*. He wants to know you're safe and that you're here because you want to be."

She eyes the phone for a long, silent moment and then reluctantly picks it up.

"2003 is the lock code."

"The year I was born," she murmurs.

And the year Nico left the family.

"You trust me with your lock code."

"I offered you freedom, Callandria. It wasn't a lie," I say, holding her gaze. "Until things are settled, you aren't to leave the house or have contact with your family. Those rules are for your safety as much as for theirs. But I'm not your captor. You aren't my prisoner. You're going to be the mother of my child."

"My father wouldn't try to hurt me, Luca," she says in disapproval.

"No, but he may try to fulfill whatever contract he sold you into." Anger sizzles in my bloodstream at the thought. "I'll start this war myself to keep that from happening, Callandria."

She swallows audibly, rattled by my confession. "Andrea Maceo," she whispers, staring down at the phone. "That's who I'm supposed to...."

"*Cristo.*" Andrea Maceo is a prick. He doesn't deserve to breathe the same air as her, let alone put his filthy hands on her gorgeous body.

"I used to have nightmares about it," she continues. "About being his wife, I mean." A soft laugh escapes her lips, devoid of humor. "Maybe he'll finally stop plaguing my dreams."

"You'll dream of me, *bella*," I say, rising to my feet to circle the table toward her as jealousy claws at my insides. Fuck. She doesn't even like the *stronzo*, and I'm pissed that he occupies her mind. That he haunts her nights. I sink my hand into her hair, craning her head back. "I'm the only man you dream about now. I'm the one you think about."

Her amber eyes lock on mine, her plump lips parted.

"When you're in my bed, I'm the only man who exists in your world," I growl.

"Am I the only woman who exists for you, Luca?" she asks. "Am I the only one you'll think about?"

My cock stiffens when jealousy flashes through her pretty eyes. Triumph surges through my veins, thoughts of Andrea Maceo forgotten at this small sign that Callandria feels something for me. It's the smallest glimmer of hope, flickering like the light of a candle, but I feel its heat.

"You doubt it, princess?" I arch a brow, reaching for my zipper with my free hand, determined to show her how completely she'll have me. I hold her gaze as I undo my pants, releasing my hard cock. "This is yours, Callandria."

Her gaze shifts from me to my cock. She whimpers, her eyes turning glassy.

"Claim it, *principessa*. Make sure the world knows who it belongs to."

"H-how?" she whispers.

I step closer, brushing the head across her lips. She whimpers again, pressing her thighs together in her chair.

"Open, *piccolina*. Let me see what heaven feels like."

She obediently parts her lips, allowing me to slip the head of my cock past them. I torment myself, dipping the tip into her mouth and then slipping it free. Over and over just to watch her perfect lips close over it.

Cristo. She's going to ruin me. I feel it in my bones. The depths I'll sink to please her. The things I'll concede to make her smile.

"Open wider," I growl, gently cupping her jaw and pushing downward with my thumb. "Let me in, *principessa*."

She opens for me, her amber eyes locked on mine, silently pleading for more. *Dio*. She's an obedient little thing when she wants to be. When she's getting what she wants. Is that the key to her heart? To give her the world? If so, I'll lay it at her feet. Whatever she wants, however she wants it.

I slip my cock past her lips, snarling curses as her hot mouth envelopes me. "Now suck, Callandria. Use your teeth. Drag them along my shaft and make me your toy. I want to feel it, princess." I want her to make it hurt. I want her to command my pleasure and my pain, to consume me. It's only fair since I intend to consume her the same way. Her world will begin and end with me.

She closes her lips around me as best she can, her eyes so dilated they're nearly black.

"*Brava ragazza*," I growl, my fist in her hair. "*Brava ragazza*." Ah, goddamn. She's the perfect little cocksucker. Her mouth is perfection, and so is she. I watch in rapt fascination as she bobs on my cock, taking me deep and then pulling back. She's shy at first, exploring and testing her limits.

And then her teeth rake down my shaft. My balls churn.

"Harder," I demand. "Make it hurt, *bella*."

Her eyes flash to mine.

"Yeah, *piccolina*," I murmur, brushing my thumb across her cheek. "You heard me. I want you to make me feel it. That fire in your soul. Give it to me, *bella*. Command me with it."

She hesitates for a moment and then gives in. Her teeth rake down my shaft again, her hand cupping my balls. I roar in pleasure and pain, caught in a net of her making. Goddamn. It's heaven, and it's hell, and I love every fucking second of it.

My grip in her hair tightens, and I rock my hips, plunging deep into her mouth. She moans around me, her eyes watering as her lips stretch to capacity. I snarl as her throat closes around me, and she chokes.

"Yes," I hiss. "Choke on my cock like a good little princess, *bella*."

Her eyes water, her face turning red. She claws at my thighs.

I pull back allowing her to breathe.

"*Voglio di più*," she gasps. *I want more.*

I curse and thrust between her lips again, giving her what she wants. She bobs on my cock, taking me deep, dragging her teeth down my shaft. Choking on me. She ruins me with her perfect mouth, *owns* me with it.

"Luca."

"Get the fuck out," I snarl at Antonio, shifting to shield Callandria from view as Antonio's voice sounds behind me.

"Marcello is at the gates."

Cazzo.

"Keep him there," I demand. "I'll be there in a minute. Now, get the fuck out."

Antonio retreats without another word.

I should stop and go speak to Marcello. Rationally, I know this. But Callandria still has my dick in her mouth. She's still looking at me with wide, dilated eyes. I still feel her rooting around in my soul, taking possession of every fucking inch of it.

I don't stop.

I pump my hips again, fucking her mouth.

She moans around me.

"We're meeting your brother with my taste on your lips," I growl. "Suck me, *bella*. Hard."

My fiery little *principessa* doesn't try to stop me. She doesn't tell me no. She hollows her cheeks and sucks, using her teeth and tongue. My balls draw up, my stomach clenching.

"I'm going to come, *piccolina*." I try to pull back, but she grabs my thighs, making it clear she wants me in her mouth. That move is enough to send me over the edge. I growl her name as cum shoots up my shaft, spilling past her lips.

Her eyes widen and then she swallows.

"Fuck," I grunt, my balls throbbing at the sight. My legs threaten to buckle as I come harder than I ever have. She takes it like the good girl she is, swallowing every drop.

I slip from her lips, gasping for breath. "*Cristo, bella. Cristo.*" I drag her out of her chair and into my arms, kissing her hard and deep. "*Mi fai impazzire.*" *You drive me crazy.*

"I know the feeling," she whispers back.

Marcello Genovese waits just outside the gates to my property, leaning against his Porsche with his arms crossed. The dark scowl on his face doesn't bode well for the impending conversation. If he brought anyone with him, though, I don't see them as I approach with Callandria at my side and Alessio and Antonio flanking us.

Callandria squeezes my hand, clearly anxious to face her brother. The similarities between them are obvious. They share the same amber eyes and Grecian features, though Marcello is over six feet tall.

Before Tommaso Genovese blew up our worlds, he and I got along well enough. We weren't necessarily good friends, but we weren't enemies either. We coexisted without malice, exchanging pleasantries whenever we crossed paths. At least, I thought we coexisted without malice between us. Perhaps I was wrong. Because he certainly said nothing when his fucking grandfather blackmailed Diego Butera into fanning the flames of war and then paid Carmine to try to kidnap Amalia.

"Easy," I murmur against Callandria's ear. "All will be well. Wait a moment, and let me speak to him."

"Luca."

"Wait, *bella*."

She huffs, and then nods reluctantly. Alessio and Antonio surround her, ensuring she's safe. If I die, I die. It is what it is. But they'll get her out of here to safety.

I don't think it'll come to that. At least not tonight. If her brother came looking for a fight, he would not have come alone. He would have come with an army. Apparently, Rafe's attempt to stall the sit-down didn't appease him. That should piss me off. Rafe is *Capo dei capi*. His word is law. Yet I appreciate the fact that Marcello cares enough about his sister to risk his life coming here to see her for himself. At least she's more than a paycheck to someone in that God-forsaken family.

"Valentino," he growls, pushing away from the Porsche as I approach the gates. His gaze shifts between me and the men guarding his sister, cold and assessing. "You really expect me to believe she's here by choice just because she walked out here holding your hand?"

"I don't really care what you believe," I say. "You showed up uninvited to my home after your family all but declared war on mine. The only reason I'm standing in front of you now is because she matters to me. You and your beliefs mean nothing."

"We declared war?" His eyebrows shoot up. "You left bodies scattered all over our fucking territory, and then the same night she disappears, a whole pile of them shows up on our doorstep."

"Tommaso Genovese killed the men scattered across your territory," I say. "We had nothing to do with that."

"Right. And I suppose your family didn't kill him, either."

"We admit full responsibility for the bodies left on Emilio's doorstep. We delivered them back to sender," I say with a shrug. "Perhaps next time your family decides to kidnap Rafe's *regina* and try to keep her from him, they'll think twice."

"And my grandfather?" Marcello growls.

"Violated the law. He's lucky he died quickly," I snap. "He wouldn't have shown the same mercy to anyone stupid enough to do the same, and you know it."

"*Cazzo*," Marcello spits, his jaw clenched. "So what now, Valentino? You punish us for his crimes by holding Callandria? You violate the law you killed him to uphold?"

"The *principessa* is precisely where she belongs," I snap back at him. "She made her choice. Ask her yourself. But if so much as a single hair on her head is harmed, I will rip your family's kingdom apart, Marcello. Nothing but rubble and a whisper of the Genovese name will remain."

"*Cristo*," he breathes. "You're in love with her."

I don't answer. It's not his business. I'm not even sure what I'd say anyway. I am in love with her. It's inexplicable, irrational, and impossible, yet it beats like a war drum in my chest anyway.

I lift my hand, gesturing for Antonio and Alessio to bring her to me. Marcello and I wait in silence for them to cross the few yards separating us.

"*Dio*," Marcello mutters under his breath when Callandria walks straight up to me.

I wrap my arm around her waist, pulling her up against my chest. My lips touch the side of her throat where I marked her earlier. Not in a show for her brother, but because she's mine. I'll touch her, kiss her whenever and wherever I damn well please.

She melts against me. And without a single word passing her lips, she confirms exactly what Marcello feared. She belongs to me now.

He eyes her silently for a long moment, perhaps looking for cracks in the facade. But there are none for him to find. Not right now. Callandria Genovese has declared her allegiance, and she's standing her ground.

She's incredible.

"*Merda*," he growls after a moment, shaking his head. "A Valentino, Callie?"

"They aren't my enemy, Marcello," she says, her soft voice clear. "They don't have to be yours either."

"They killed Grandfather."

"I know," Callandria whispers.

"You know." Marcello shakes his head. "And still you stand here in *his* arms?"

"Would you rather me live in misery with Andrea Maceo like an obedient little princess, Marcello?" she snaps. "That's the future that waits for me at home. I'm nothing more than chattel to be sold to the men in our family, and you know it."

"That's not true."

"No? When did you ever step out of line to stop what they were doing, Marcello? You knew long before I did what my future held, but you said nothing." She laughs abruptly. "You told me that's the way it had to be."

Marcello flinches, guilt flickering through his expression. "What would you have had me do, Callie? Kill our grandfather and father?"

"Of course not," she says. "But don't stand here now and act as though I betrayed our family when I was never more than a pawn and a paycheck to the Genovese family."

"And Mom? Grandma? What am I supposed to tell them?" Marcello asks.

You tell them that I'm safe," she says, her voice trembling. "And you tell them that I'm exactly where I need to be."

Need. Not want, but need. *Dio*. She still isn't sure this is what she wants, that I'm who she wants. Physically, she's ready. But mentally and emotionally, she's still at war with herself.

That's not acceptable to me. Until every piece of her belongs to me, I won't take her to my bed. It's the only choice I have left to offer her.

"And you tell our father that I'm living life on my own terms from now on," she says. "I decide what happens to me and what alliances I form for the family. I'm not property to be sold to the highest bidder. If there's an heir, it will be because *I* chose it. My child will be a Valentino."

"*Cazzo*," Marcello hisses, shocked.

"Go home, Marcello," Callandria says. "And talk our father out of whatever desperate plot he's trying to form before he gets us all killed. Let Grandfather's God-forsaken war die with him."

Chapter Seven

CALLANDRIA

I pace around Luca's bedroom, restless and out of sorts. I didn't expect Marcello to show up tonight, though perhaps I should have. My father may be willing to play by the rules, but Marcello isn't so easily convinced. He's my older brother, my best friend. We've always been close.

And yet nothing I said tonight was untrue. He knew long before I did that I was expected to marry Andrea Maceo. He never said anything to me about it. He let me grow up believing I had a future outside of this world. I understand why he did it, but that doesn't change the fact that the one person I trusted the most has always and will always put the family above me.

Isn't that the way it always goes for Made men? *La Cosa Nostra* above all things. And yet this had nothing to do with *mafioso* business, not really. He spoke no vow that held his tongue when it came to confessing the truth about my future. But he held his tongue anyway. He treated me as less than, just like Tommaso Genovese did. Just like my father did.

The stark contrast between my own family and Luca Valentino has never been more apparent than it is right now. Luca may not tell me everything, but he's been honest with me. Even when he knows the truth is brutal and ugly, he gives it to me. He doesn't keep me in the dark, waiting for the other shoe to drop.

"Thank you," I blurt, whirling to face him.

"For what, *bella*?" he asks, eyeing me from the bed where he's lounging. He's fully dressed, though he kicked his shoes off. His hands rest over his stomach, his feet crossed. He looks perfectly at ease, and yet his eyes are a million miles away.

"For letting me see Marcello."

"You don't owe me thanks." His eyes clear as he focuses on me. "You're upset."

"No," I lie.

"Liar."

"He annoyed me," I mutter with a defensive shrug.

"Ah. So I'm not the only one who breaks your boxes." His lips twitch. "Come here, *bella*."

"Why?" I ask, suddenly wary.

"You're annoyed with your brother. I want to make it better." He crooks a finger, beckoning me toward the bed. "I promise not to remove your clothes."

I slowly creep toward him, surprised by his willingness to let me remain clothed. "You're very confusing, Luca Valentino," I mutter when he hooks his arms around my waist, pulling me onto the bed with him.

"How so?"

I shrug noncommittally.

"Tell me, *principessa*."

"You're letting me keep my clothes," I whisper.

He smiles, his expression soft. "How many times do I have to tell you, Callandria? I won't force you to give yourself to me. I take only what you give me of your own free will." He tucks hair behind my ears. "And you aren't ready to give me every piece of you."

"Oh." I'm not entirely sure what he means by every piece of me, but I have a feeling he isn't just talking about my body. This man is...complicated. Like the impossible nine-piece puzzles. Everyone assumes the ones with more pieces are harder to figure out, but they're wrong.

Those nine small, oddly shaped pieces leave nearly everyone confused as they frantically try to figure out how they fit together. Most give up without ever getting anywhere. This man is exactly like that. Impossible to figure out. Confusing. Made of sharp edges and angles that somehow snap together to form an image few ever actually manage to complete.

"I like seeing you in my shirt, *bella*," he murmurs after a moment.

"The shirts you bought me are too small."

"Hmm. I wonder how that happened."

I peek up at him. "You bought them on purpose, didn't you?"

"You look good in my shirt." He shrugs, unrepentant.

"Luca," I groan, and then I smile, unable to help myself. He really is a wicked man. He plays by his own rules. Actually, I think he makes his own rules as he goes. He does what he wants when he wants and makes no apologies for it. I want to know what freedom like that tastes like.

"Sleep, *bella*," he murmurs, dragging me halfway on top of him.

"I'm not tired."

"No?"

I shake my head, a blush staining my cheeks.

"What do you want to do, hmm?"

"I don't know," I whisper. It's a lie. I know exactly what I want to do. I want to pick up where we left off before my brother interrupted us. But he already said we aren't doing that. So I don't know where that leaves me. Frustrated and horny, I supposed.

His hand slips down my back. "You really shouldn't sleep fully clothed."

"Why not?"

"It's not good for you."

"Since when?"

"Since I can't fucking touch any part of you that I want to touch, *bella*," he growls, flipping me onto my back. He follows me over, hovering over me on his forearms. He presses his face to my throat, breathing me in. "*Merda*. You drive me crazy."

"I know the feeling, Luca."

"Yeah?" His gaze flicks to mine, ravenous. "Do you, Callandria? The things I want to do to you..." He dips his head again, skimming his lips across my breasts. "When you're mine, you'll come to love the chains, *principessa*. You'll plead with me to put you in them and take what I want from you."

"Luca," I groan, arching toward his mouth.

"I'll know every fantasy you have, every sensitive spot on your body." He bites my nipple, pulling a cry from my lips. "I'm going to ruin you, princess. Just like you ruined me."

"I didn't r-ruin you," I gasp.

"Liar," he says, prowling down my body. "As soon as I fucking set eyes on you, you ruined me, Callandria." He tugs my shirt up so his lips land against my belly. He bites me there, leaving another mark on my skin. "*Non faccio che pensare a te.*" All I think about is you.

"Luca," I whimper. "Please."

"Let me see what belongs to me, *piccolina*," he breathes. "Let me taste it."

"Yes. Please, yes," I sob in relief, so tangled up in desire, I think I'd hand him the keys to my soul if he wanted them right now. He wants every piece of me. And God help me, I want to give them to him because he's all I think about too. It's terrifying but it's true. The last twenty-four hours of my life have been some of the best hours of my life. I've never felt more like myself and less like myself at the same time.

He groans, dragging his teeth down my abdomen. My muscles quiver beneath his touch, my body reacting to him on a cellular level. I feel him everywhere, as if he's pumping through my veins. He hooks his thumbs into my pants. I lift my hips, allowing him to drag them and my panties down my hips.

"*Bellissima*," he breathes, his eyes locked on the wet, needy flesh between my legs. "Oh, *principessa*. I'm going to have so much fun with you."

He presses his nose to my center, breathing me in.

"Luca," I cry, shocked. Turned on. Embarrassed. I hardly know which I feel.

"*Perfezione*." He lifts his head to look at me, his expression stark with need. Eyes black with desire. He's never looked more dangerous to me. Or more beautiful. This is the ruthless, brutal man willing to kill to keep me. The one who would commit atrocities to avenge me. This is...*Dio*. This is the man I'm falling in love with.

He spreads my legs, fitting himself between them. My pants still dangle from one leg, but I don't think he notices. His eyes lock on mine, holding me captive as he bends his head. He never breaks my gaze as he splits me open with two fingers and presses a hot kiss directly to my clit.

My hips jolt from the bed as pleasure stabs into me.

He wraps his free arm around me, ruthlessly dragging me back down beneath him. "No," he growls. "You stay right here, *piccolina*. Let me take you to heaven this time."

"Luca, please," I sob, clawing at the bedsheets. "Please!"

"Please, what? More?" He runs his tongue around my clit. "Less?" He drags each lower lip into his mouth, sucking my juices from them. "Never stop?" He torments me, taking long, languid licks of me. "Never give you up? Please, what, *bella*?"

"Make me come!" I cry, desperate for it. Willing to beg and plead for it. "Please, Luca."

"As you command, *principessa*," he breathes. I thought he was eating me before, but I was wrong. So wrong. He falls on me like a man brought to the edge of madness, consumed by the meal in front of him. He's everywhere at once, playing my body as if he knows exactly how to make it sing. And God, it does. *I* do.

My cries fill the room, echoing in the corners like a carnal aria.

"That's it, *bella*," he murmurs against my flesh. "Scream for me."

My voice breaks on his name as the pleasure splits me asunder and scatters me to the winds. I float away, riding on waves of bliss unlike anything I've ever felt before. He doesn't stop or let up until my field of vision goes black and my heart threatens to stop entirely, frozen in this one perfect moment of peace.

I float back to Earth, landing safely in his arms.

"Callandria," he breathes. "*Mia bella principessa.*"

I know I'm dreaming as soon as I find myself outside. The city is crumbling. Blood flows like a river down the streets. Bodies still lay where they fell, bloodied and battered.

"No," I whisper, shaking my head. This isn't supposed to happen. Luca and I are supposed to stop this. We're on the same side.

Luca.

No. Oh, no.

I turn in a frantic circle, trying to figure out where I am. Close to my father's house. I take off running in that direction, praying I get there in time this time, that I save

Luca before it's too late. My lungs burn as I race down the sidewalk, heedlessly running through the bones that litter the city in a macabre display.

I dodge fallen bodies, biting my tongue to keep from sobbing at the sight of them. There are so many. So much death. So much destruction. *Dio.* This isn't supposed to happen.

I trip at the corner, nearly falling on my face before I catch myself. My ankle throbs as I skid onto my father's street, my eyes already scanning for Luca.

I cry out in horror when my eyes fall on the row of bodies spread across the middle of the street. Marcello. My father. Luca. All dead.

"No!" I scream, falling to my knees. "No!"

"Callandria." Rough hands grab me, shaking me awake.

I sit up with a sharp cry, scrabbling backward in terror. And then my gaze lands on Luca, his mocha eyes filled with worry as he stares down at me. He's alive. I sob in relief, flinging myself at his chest.

"Luca," I gasp, hitting him like a cannonball.

"Easy, *bella*, easy," he croons, wrapping me up in his arms. "It was just a dream."

Except it wasn't. Just like this morning, it was a glimpse into one possible future. One too awful to comprehend or even put into words. My family, dead. Luca, dead. The whole city bleeding. How am I supposed to stop that? I don't know, but I have to stop it.

I can't lose him. Not now. I just found him.

"Talk to me, *piccolina*," he says. "What haunts your mind?"

"You were dead," I whisper. "So was Marcello and my f-father. The city was destroyed. There were bodies everywhere." I shudder in horror, pressing my face to his throat. "It was awful, Luca."

"You dreamed of losing me."

"Yes."

"And this is why you were screaming my name?"

"I...I was screaming your name?"

"Yes."

"Yes," I whisper.

"*Piccolina*," he says softly, pressing his lips to my crown. He holds me for a long time just like that, neither of us speaking. And then he sighs quietly and tips my face up to his, brushing his thumbs beneath my eyes to collect tears I didn't know I'd shed. "I'll never deserve you, Callandria, but I'll fight like hell to keep you anyway."

Chapter Eight

LUCA

The next two days pass in peace. We don't hear a peep from the Genovese family, and they don't hear shit from us. I spend my days making plans with Rafe and Mattia in case Emilio decides to do anything rash and my nights with Callandria.

We touch and explore. I teach her just how much she loves my wicked mouth. She owns me with hers. But I don't push. I don't rush her. I fucking can't. She hasn't realized it yet, but she's in love with me. It's fragile and new, as easily lost as her growing trust in me. I refuse to give up either easily.

Late on day two, Emilio demands a sit-down for the following morning. He won't be put off anymore. Rumors are beginning to spread, and his hold on the Genovese empire is precarious.

"Fuck," I growl into the phone when Rafe delivers the news. "Fine. I'll do it. But Callandria won't be there. And if he insults her, he does so at his own peril."

"You're in love with her," my older brother says. There is no surprise in his voice, no judgment.

I hesitate to tell him anyway, unwilling to let her or my feelings for her be used as ammunition in whatever is coming our way. As head of the family, Rafe doesn't always have a choice. He does what he has to do because he must.

"I'll take your silence as an answer," he says dryly. "Does she know?"

Does she? Perhaps. I've certainly tried to show her, but I haven't spoken the words. I've been waiting...for what? I don't know. *Dio*. I'm an idiot. I want her heart but haven't given her assurance that she has mine. She dreams of losing me, but I keep my truth guarded, waiting for her to give me every piece of her soul.

She already has mine, but does she know that? The possibility that she doesn't is worrisome.

"I have to go," I mutter to Rafe.

"Be here in the morning, Luca," he reminds me. "We'll meet him at the deli."

"Fine." I disconnect and go in search of Callandria.

I find her in the kitchen with Ricardo, Antonio, and Alessio, playing poker. Judging by the disgruntled looks on Antonio and Alessio's faces and the pile of chips in front of her, she's not losing.

"How much do they owe you, *bella*?" I ask, stepping up behind her to examine the cards in her hand. She has a pair of fours. The rest of her hand is shit.

"I stopped counting a while ago," she says cheerfully. "I'm not sure they've ever played this game before, Luca."

Antonio grunts.

I chuckle as Alessio's lips purse like he just tasted something sour. They've probably been playing poker for longer than she's been alive.

Callandria tosses a three into the discard pile. "Hit me, please," she asks Antonio.

He slides another card across the table to her.

She peeks at it and laughs to herself before tossing another $100 chip into the center of the table. The card is a five. Completely useless with the hand she has, but her bluff works.

Alessio dabs sweat from his brow.

"I fold," Ricardo says, tossing his cards down on the table. "I know when my old ass is beaten."

"Me too," Alessio mutters in disgust, tossing his cards down.

Antonio eyes his cards and then Callandria, who simply smiles at him. "Fuck it," he growls. "I'm out too."

"*Sei coniglios*," I say, laughing at all three of them.

"*Vaffanculo*," Antonio mutters without heat. "You try playing against her. She's *una principessa spietata*."

"Show them your cards, *bella*."

She lays her cards out on the table, showing her hand.

Ricardo laughs, slapping the table.

"*Cristo*," Alessio mutters.

Antonio merely looks at me as if to say 'See? She's ruthless.'

"Who taught you to play, *piccolina*?" I ask her as she scoops her chips into a pile, humming quietly.

"Marcello and my bodyguards. I hounded them when I was little until they taught me everything they know," she says.

I nod, satisfied with her answer. Judging by Alessio and Antonio's expressions, they didn't ask. "You assume because she's a *principessa* that she grew up in some bubble or that she's delicate," I say quietly. "You know nothing. A *principessa's* spine is forged from steel and covered in diamonds. She's the most dangerous person in any room she walks into because she's the smartest and she's willing to risk the most. Her survival depends on it. Don't ever forget that again."

Alessio and Antonio nod their understanding. Even Ricardo bobs his head, looking at Callandria with a new appreciation.

We fight with guns and knives and underhanded deals. They live in the same world we do, and they need none of that to survive it. When they're required to fight, they do it with their brains and sheer force of will. They aren't delicate. They aren't helpless. We don't protect them because they're weak. We defend them because they're the most deserving of all of us. Protecting our women is an honor. One any single Made man worthy of the name would die for without hesitation.

"Come, *bella*," I murmur, holding out my hand to her. "I think you've won enough of their money for one night."

"Oh, I'm not keeping it," she says.

"Yes, you are. Maybe next time they'll think twice before underestimating you because you're a woman."

"Luca, really," she protests.

"Hush, *bella*. It's your money now."

"So that means I can do what I want with it, right?"

"Anything except give it back to my men," I agree.

"Fine." She gathers up her chips before shoving them into my hands. "This is for you," she says. "Please put it toward Mrs. Ricardo's care. Oh. And also toward whatever you're paying Alessio and Antonio to protect me." She pats me on the chest, beaming at me.

"*Cazzo*," I growl as she sails past me out of the kitchen, satisfied with herself.

All three of the men at the table look at me with the exact same expression.

"Don't even say it," I growl. "Not a fucking word."

Alessio actually cracks a smile.

I curse and stomp out of the room after Callandria, pretty sure I walked right into that one myself. *Dio*. She's too smart for her own good, and she's fearless.

Yes, I love her. So much I can't fucking think about anything but her since she entered my life. She's the only thing that matters.

By the time I make it upstairs, she's already in the bedroom. I stop in the doorway, drinking in the sight of her bathed in the moonlight filtering in through the windows. It lights her with an ethereal glow.

"Did you mean what you said down there?" she asks without turning to look at me. "Do you really think *principessas* are everything you said?"

I stride into the room, pushing the door closed with my foot before I deposit her chips on the dresser. "I know one who is," I answer.

"Who?"

"I'm looking at her, *bella*." I strip my shirt off over my head, joining her in front of the windows. "You dropped me to my knees without even lifting a hand against me."

"Oh, I lifted one," she says, smiling.

"Yeah, you did." I drag her back against my chest, pressing my lips to her ear. "That's the moment I fell in love with you."

"Luca," she gasps.

"I've been waiting for you to give every piece of yourself to me, but I'm an idiot," I murmur. "I never told you that you already have every piece of me. I'll wait as long as it takes for you to find room in your heart for me, too."

"What if..." She turns her head to look up at me. "What if you're already there, Luca?"

"Don't say it if you don't mean it, *bella*," I whisper...plead. *Cristo*. Yes, I plead. Because I won't fucking survive if she changes her mind later and tries to kick me out of her heart. I need her. More than air or water or fucking life.

She's the one thing in this world that makes it worth saving. That makes *me* worth saving. My brothers and I...we're damned. But this *bella principessa* makes me feel like there's some hope for a future that isn't bleak. There's hope for salvation. This world doesn't have to be destruction and devastation. We don't have to dismantle to win. We can build. *We can be rebuilt.*

And if I still get cast into hell, at least I'll go knowing what it means to be complete. I'll go knowing what it's like to hold the world in my arms and see forever in her eyes.

She's my soul, the one thing in this world that brings me peace. The only fucking thing that gives me hope.

I need her to survive.

"Don't say it if you don't mean it," I whisper again.

She turns in my arms, placing her palm against my cheek. Her amber sirens' eyes meet mine, dragging me even deeper under her spell. "*Ti amo*, Luca," she breathes, the words so soft I strain to hear them. But my heart does. Fuck. My heart does.

"*Cristo*," I growl, wrapping her hair in my fist. I crane her head back, tugging until her eyes darken. "Say it again, *bella*."

"*Ti amo*."

"Again."

"*Ti amo*."

She means it. The truth is painted across every beautiful line of her face. It spills from her eyes in two drops, making tracks down her round cheeks. She's mine. Finally, this beautiful little princess is mine.

I drag her into my arms, pressing my mouth to hers in fervent devotion. I taste her tears on my lips and claim them as mine. God made perfection when he crafted her. Sweet enough to soften this world, fierce enough to survive it, brave enough to conquer it. A *principessa* to her core.

I tug the top of her t-shirt aside, planting my lips against the side of her neck as my hands roam down her body, exploring every lush curve.

We work together to strip her, leaving her in nothing but the moonlight shining through the windows and the glow of the lamp behind us.

"Place your hands on the glass, *bella*."

She lifts them slowly, trembling like the sweetest little lamb. I nuzzle her throat, nipping at her collarbone. She's been using my soap, but she smells sweet there, as if not even my scent masks the essence of her.

My thumbs roll over her hard nipples, earning a throaty moan from her. I pinch, tweaking them just enough to make it sting.

"Luca!" she sobs, her hands slipping on the glass. She arches into my hands, silently pleading for more.

"You like a little pain too, *bella*."

"Yes."

I smile. It wasn't a question. I know she does. I've been learning her. What she likes. What makes her go wild for me. What makes her come so hard she can't move. She likes being pinned down. She likes pain.

My princess is a dirty little thing.

I always wondered why nothing ever appealed to me. No kink I saw, no show I watched. None of it held my interest because it wasn't *her*. She's my favorite flavor, my guilty pleasure. She's the itch I could never scratch. Everything about her is exactly what I searched for and never could find. I wasn't looking for a quick fuck. All that time, I was looking for *her*. Callandria. The other half of my soul.

I turn my head, requesting Alexa turn off the lights. A second later, the room goes dark, leaving us in nothing but moonlight.

"Watch us in the window, *bella*," I whisper in her ear. "See what I do to this perfect body."

"Luca."

"Watch," I growl, swatting her right breast.

She cries out in shock, the sound quickly fading to a moan. Yes, she likes a little pain. She likes it all too well. I can smell how much she likes it.

I press my lips to her throat again, kissing and biting as I play with her nipples, pinching and twisting, teasing until she's sobbing and wetness glistens on her thighs.

"Now, touch your pussy, *piccolina*. Spread your lips and let me see it."

She whimpers, removing one hand from the window to do as instructed. Her chest heaves as she slips her hand between her legs, parting her folds for me.

Even in the window, her cunt is perfect.

"Play with yourself, *bella*."

"I..."

I swat her other breast. "Stop thinking, *principessa*. In this room, your body is mine. I'll touch it how I want. Fuck you how I want. Trust me to take care of you."

She exhales a breath.

"If something is too much, you say stop, and it stops. Understand?"

"Yes."

"Then give me what I want."

She rolls her thumb over her clit, gasping.

"*Brava ragazza*," I breathe. Fuck. She's perfect in every way. I'll fight like hell to be worthy of her, to be a man deserving of her.

I watch her in the window as she touches herself, her eyes riveted on the way her hand moves between her legs. On the way her stomach muscles quiver, and her thick thighs tremble. On how her chest heaves. She's so fucking sexy. *Cristo*. She's realizing for the first time just how beautiful her body is. She's going to wreck me with that knowledge, bring me to my fucking knees with it.

"My turn," I growl, sliding my hand around her waist to cover hers. I drag her hand toward her opening, circling her tight little hole. She's so wet. Goddamn. She's horny for it. "Let me see your fingers, *bella*."

I link our hands together and guide her fingers to her hole. We work together, slowly working them into her. "Now, fuck yourself with them."

She whimpers, shaking in my arms. But she obeys. The wet sound of her fingers reaches my ears as she pushes them in and out of her cunt. I run my thumb over her clit, watching her in the mirror, feeling every single thrust of her palm against mine.

I groan, pressing my finger to her opening, too, unable to resist. "Let me in, *piccolina*. Let me feel what you're doing to yourself."

She whines my name.

I push the tip of my finger inside her. Ah, goddamn. She's tight. I bury my face in her throat, snarling curses as I work my finger in deeper.

"Luca," she whispers. "*Dio Santo*, Luca."

"Let me feel it, *bella*," I growl. "Fuck your fingers."

She groans, slipping her fingers partway out before pushing them back in again. They press against mine. She's so goddamn tight.

Her breath grows choppy, each thrust of her fingers pulling a moan from her lips. Beads of sweat trickle between my shoulders.

"Curl them up," I instruct, moving my finger over hers to show her what I mean. I curl hers upward, guiding them toward her G-spot. I press hers to it, stroking firmly.

She goes rigid in my arms, her mouth opening on a choked cry. Her inner muscles clamp down around our fingers, and she shatters.

What little restraint I possess snaps. I spin her around, pressing her back to the glass, and drop to my knees in front of her. One of her legs drapes over my shoulder, opening her up to me.

I press my hand to her stomach to keep her in place...and swoop. She screams, shoving her hands into my hair as I attack her with my mouth, growling my pleasure against her soaked folds. Her taste floods my mouth. I go back again and again, drinking her down like ambrosia.

She sobs, wailing my name, yanking at my hair. She fights like a little hellcat as I eat her from one orgasm directly into another, not giving her a second to rest or breathe. I can't. *Cristo.* I fucking can't.

"Mine," I snarl, sucking on her clit. "This is mine, Callandria."

"Yes, yes," she sobs. "It's yours, Luca. It's all yours. Oh, God, please. Please!" Her voice cracks as she shatters again.

Her legs collapse.

I catch her, dragging her down into my lap. She deserves a bed for her first time, but I'm too far gone to get us there. I lean forward, dragging the duvet cover onto the floor to offer her some protection, and then lay her out on it.

"I can't wait," I growl, dragging my pants halfway down my legs before yanking her thighs up around my waist. My cock lands against her center. "*Cristo, bella. Perdonami.*"

"*Ti amo*, Luca. *Ti amo*," she breathes.

I thrust into her, taking her mouth in a deep kiss. She cries out in shock, clawing down my back as her body stretches around me, her virgin barrier shredding.

"*Perdonami*," I whisper against her lips, writhing in ecstasy. Fuck. She feels like heaven. I fight to stay still, desperately trying to give her time to adjust.

But she's moving beneath me, squirming around, writhing. Every move she makes seats me deeper, leaving me reeling in pleasure more intense than anything I've ever felt.

I groan in surrender and give in to it, driving my hips into hers. She throws her head back, moaning. Ah, goddamn. She loves it. The pleasure. The pain. The fact that I'm inside her. Ecstasy swirls through her amber eyes and stains her cheeks.

"*Brava ragazza*," I growl, thrusting my hand into her thick mass of hair. I angle her head, kissing her again. And then again.

We kiss and fuck and moan, lost in rapture together. I'm rough with her, pounding into her like a man brought to the edge of madness. She claws my back and bites me, fierce in her pleasure. We're gentle, too, holding each other close, gasping words of love and devotion.

"This is us, *bella*," I rasp. "This is what we are together. This is who we are."

"Yes," she whispers, her back bowing from the floor. "Luca."

"Callandria."

She reaches for me, her dilated eyes fixed on mine. "*Sempre*."

I press my forehead to hers as the base of my spine begins to tingle. "*Sempre, principessa. Sempre.*"

She'll have every piece of me, always. It was always meant to be hers. I was always meant to be hers. Not a fucking thing on this earth can change it now. I won't allow it.

She moans my name, her body going rigid as her orgasm strikes. It washes over her in a flood, lighting her up like the queen she is. I growl her name, pounding into her without rhythm until the cord snaps, and I follow her over the edge, filling her full of me.

And when I collapse beside her, I send up a prayer that my seed takes, and my kid grows in her womb. Not to form an alliance between our families. Not to stop a war. But because I want to watch this woman, the one I live and breathe for, grow round with my child.

Chapter Nine

CALLANDRIA

"You're going to meet my father," I say, staring at Luca as my stomach churns uncomfortably. This was not the start to the morning I envisioned. After last night, I kind of hoped for a repeat performance. Not...this.

"I have to go, *bella*," he says gently. "He's getting impatient. If I don't meet him, he may do something foolish."

"Meeting him is foolish," I mutter, crossing my arms to scowl at him. "Your family just killed his father and took his daughter. We cost him the Maceo fortune. I doubt he's feeling very rational right now, Luca."

"And he'll feel less so if his power is undermined because his people don't think he's doing anything," Luca says. "All will be well."

I snort, not sure I believe that. How can I when I'm plagued by dreams that warn me otherwise? We haven't stopped the war yet. We've only delayed what feels inevitable. I'm not ready to lose him. I don't want to lose Marcello or my father, either. Perhaps that's selfish of me, to want to keep all of the men in my life, but it's what I want, regardless.

"*Bella ragazza*," Luca murmurs, pulling me into his arms. His lips brush my forehead. "Trust me. All will be well."

"It better be, Luca Valentino," I growl, scowling at him to keep myself from crying. "I'm going to be furious with you if anything happens to you."

"Yeah?" His hand slides down my back before he grips my ass hard, pulling me into him. His lust-filled eyes settle on mine, burning hot. "Don't give me reasons to play with fire, *principessa*. You know how much I like getting on your nerves."

I sniff at him, filling the sound with as much disdain as I can muster. "*Bastardo*."

His wicked, wanton smirk makes my knees weak. "When you're chained to my bed tonight and I'm taking what I want from you, you'll see just how much of a bastard I can be, princess." He nips my throat, his teeth driving me close to heaven. "You can fight if you want, Callandria. We both know how much I like it when you do."

I moan, my core clenching as a hot rush of desire pulses through me. What is this man doing to me? I hardly recognize the desperate, wicked woman he's turned me into. Yet I've never felt freer. This is who I was meant to be. Luca's queen. His lover. The other half of his soul.

He pulls me toward the dark, and I hold him in the light. We're not king and captive, conqueror and conquered. We're evenly matched. *Principessa* and underboss. We're *destino*.

I've never been happier. Even though our world is nowhere near steady in its orbit, I feel centered in a way I never have.

For the first time in my life, I feel...hope. It flutters in my chest like the fragile wings of a butterfly. Every hour with him, it grows stronger. Even with the sword hanging over our heads, I feel *alive*.

I can't lose that now. I can't lose him.

"Please be careful," I whisper, pressing my face to his chest. His heart beats beneath my ear, strong and steady. "Come back to me."

"*Sempre*," he promises. His lips touch mine in a gentle kiss. "*Ti amo, bella.*"

"*Ti amo*, Luca."

Once Luca and Antonio leave, I hang out in the kitchen with Ricardo and Alessio. They refuse to play poker with me again.

"You aren't visiting your wife today?" I ask Ricardo, watching as he builds a house of cards with surprisingly nimble hands.

"I'll go later," he says.

My brows pull down. "Luca asked you to hang around to help babysit, didn't he?" I guess.

Ricardo chuckles. "I don't believe he put it quite that way, no."

I grumble under my breath. Of course Luca asked him to stay. He usually leaves Antonio and Alessio with me.

"Why doesn't he have more men?" I ask Alessio.

"Doesn't want them." Alessio shrugs.

"Why not?"

"Ask him."

I huff. Getting Alessio to engage in conversation is a study in frustration. The man rarely speaks more than a word or two at a time. I know he has more to say though. I always see it lurking behind his eyes. There's an entire world going on in there. He simply chooses not to share it. It's mildly infuriating because I like to know things.

"Does Gabriel have more men?"

"No."

"Why not?"

Alessio's lips twitch. "You ask a lot of questions, *principessa*."

"And you answer none of them."

"Gabriel has himself," he says with a shrug. "It's what he prefers. Ask him why."

Well, I suppose that's better than nothing.

Alessio stands abruptly. "I need to go check the property." His unyielding gaze settles on me. "Stay here, please."

"Yes, sir," I retort sarcastically, saluting him. I didn't plan on leaving the kitchen anyway. Antonio usually checks the property every hour, but I guess since he's not here, the task falls to Alessio. I don't intend to make his job more difficult.

I've been a model…whatever I am. I'm no longer even sure. I'm not a captive, but I'm not free to leave yet, either. We're in limbo, waiting for my father to decide whether he's willing to bend his knee.

Please, God, let him bend, I pray. It's the only way this whole nightmare ends with a whimper instead of a roar. It's the only way all three of them—my father, Luca, and Marcello—survive.

Alessio shakes his head at me, humor in his gaze, and then strides from the kitchen. I watch Ricardo for several long moments, fascinated by how quickly and efficiently he grows his little tower of cards.

A simple breeze would knock it over, yet he builds it anyway, with all the patience of a man who has all day.

"Aren't you worried it'll collapse?" I ask after a moment.

"Not everything is meant to be permanent, *cara*," he says. "There's beauty in impermanence too. Sometimes, we're simply meant to enjoy the building while it lasts."

His words strike a raw nerve, one far too easily agitated. My stomach twists uncomfortably. Are Luca and I building a house of cards, one that was always destined to collapse? Is that what my dreams have been trying to tell me?

No. I don't believe that. I *won't* believe that.

"How..." I lick my lips. "How do you know the difference, Ricardo? Between what's meant to be permanent and what's supposed to fall apart?"

"You listen to your heart, *principessa*." Ricardo looks up from his cards and smiles at me, his kind eyes crinkling at the corners. "It'll guide you."

I bob my head in a distracted nod, staring through the maze of diamonds that make up his house. He's right. Luca told Alessio and Antonio last night that a *principessa's* greatest weapon is her mind, but he was wrong. It's her heart. We survive by trusting our instincts and letting them guide us. And mine have been telling me for days that Luca is my destiny. They've also been telling me that this isn't over. We haven't won.

My father isn't going to agree to an alliance with the Valentino family so long as he believes an alliance between the Genovese and Maceo families is still possible. His honor won't allow him to do so. In that way, he's just like my grandfather. Too proud for his own good. Too stubborn for anyone else's. Luca and Rafe need to talk to Alessandro Maceo before they meet my father.

"Can I use your phone, Ricardo?" I ask.

He glances over at me.

"It's important," I say. "I need to talk to Luca. You can call him yourself if you don't trust me. I just need to speak to him before he gets to..."

The breath rushes from my lungs in a strangled whistle as Marcello appears at the patio door, a gun in his hand and blood dripping from his hand. He presses his fingers to his lips to silence me, and aims the weapon at Ricardo.

"No!" I shout, shoving Ricardo as hard as I can.

The elderly man lists to the side in his chair and then topples out of it. His house of cards wobbles and then falls. Cards float to the floor, scattering around Ricardo as the back glass shatters.

I scream again, throwing myself to the floor with my hands over my head. My heart pounds against my ribcage as glass rains down around us, bouncing off the cobblestones.

"Goddammit, Callie!" Marcello roars into the chaos, the sound of his steps rushing toward me. "I almost shot you." He grabs me, yanking me up by the arms. "*Cristo*. Are you all right?"

"I'm fine!" I snap, slapping his hands away from me. "What are you doing here? You tried to shoot Ricardo!" Oh my God. Ricardo. I jerk away from my brother, scrambling to my feet to check on Ricardo.

He's lying prostrate on the floor, blood oozing from a gash on his forehead. His face is pale, his eyes closed. But he's breathing.

Dio, he's breathing.

"I would have shot him if you hadn't pushed him out of the way. What the fuck were you thinking?" Marcello growls from behind me.

"You were going to shoot an innocent man?" I spin to face him, horrified. "He's in his eighties, Marcello!"

"And he's helping that *figlio di puttana* hold you here against your will," Marcello spits. "He deserves death, *sorella*."

My stomach sinks. "What did you do to Alessio, Marcello?"

He clenches his jaw, refusing to answer.

"Tell me!" I shout, shoving him hard. "Where is Alessio?"

"I left him where he fell."

"You killed him," I whisper in horror.

"He was still breathing when I walked away." His eyes flash with malice. "It's more than he deserves."

"*Dio Santo*!" I growl, throwing my hands up. "I'm not here against my will, you big idiot. This is *exactly* where I want to be."

"You don't mean that, Callie."

"Yes, I do!" I cry. "I'm in love with him, Marcello. How do you not understand that?"

"*Cazzo*," Marcello whispers, his confident expression slipping. "You don't mean that."

"Yes, I do. So just go home. You've done enough damage for one day. *Dio*, out of everyone, I thought you would understand how I could love him," I say, dashing tears from my cheeks. "You hate this world just as much as he does. Except he's the only one trying to drag our families from the brink of war. You're hellbent on tipping us into one."

"How?" Marcello demands. "How does all of this possibly drag us from the brink of war, Callie? They've decimated our numbers. They've undermined his position. And now they've jeopardized our alliance with the Maceo family."

"An alliance paid for with *my* flesh," I snap in defiance. "He freed me from being prostituted to increase the Genovese fortune and position. That's what you meant to say, Marcello. That's the truth of what he did. He gave me a choice about matters that impact *my* life, *my* future, and those of any children I have. And he offers his own fortune in place of theirs. The Maceo fortune doesn't even compare to what Luca offers, and you know it."

Marcello clenches his jaw, stubbornly refusing to admit that I'm right even though we both know I am. He's too intractable for his own good.

"Just go, Marcello," I say sadly. "And don't come back here again. I may be able to protect you this time, but he'll kill you next time, and I won't be able to stop him." As much as I love my brother, I'm not even sure I could try to protect him if he tries to get to me like this again. I made my choice. I belong with Luca now. I can't ask him to stand aside and let my brother taunt him and attack his people on his own property.

"I'm not leaving without you, Callie."

"Well, I'm not going with you," I say, exasperated. "And if you're here when Luca gets home, he will kill you."

Something flickers through his expression, the same thing I saw the other night when I reminded him that he wasn't innocent in allowing me to be sold like chattel. Guilt. I've known him my whole life. I can read him. And what I read in his eyes now makes my blood run cold. He's hiding something.

"Tell me," I growl. "Now, Marcello."

"The sit-down is a setup, Callie," he says quietly. "Father is in too deep with the Maceo family. He's been borrowing against your marriage contract for years. If I don't show up at home with you in the next hour, he's going to kill Luca."

"No," I whisper, shaking my head. "No." Even as I speak the denial, I see the truth in his gaze. The pity. He's not lying to me. My father is going to kill Luca to get me back.

I was never free. We never won. Like Ricardo's house of cards, we were impermanent, destined to fall.

"I'll go," I mumble, my soul screaming in pain. Whatever it takes to keep Luca alive...that's what I'll do. I have no choice. I'd rather live a thousand lifetimes knowing he's safe and I can't have him than to live a single one where he's gone and I have to pick up the pieces.

Sacrifice. That's what it means to be a *principessa*. That's our destiny.

Chapter Ten

LUCA

"Mind your temper, Luca," Rafe mutters as we pull up in front of the deli midway between Valentino and Genovese territory. At least, it looks like a deli. It's nothing more than a front for these fucking meetings. Neutral ground. At least it used to be.

I suppose Genovese probably wouldn't see it that way if he knew Rafe shot Tommaso inside before having the place scrubbed of all evidence.

"I'll mind my temper so long as he minds his fucking mouth," I mutter to my brother. "He insults my future wife at his own peril."

Emilio Genovese is a boorish, insolent prick on a good day. He always has been. If he lacks the good sense to treat his daughter with respect, I'll respond as he deserves. She's endured enough because of him. Selling her into a marriage contract as a child. It's a disgusting, shameful practice that should have died out long ago. She isn't property to be bartered and sold. No woman is.

"I should have brought more weapons," Antonio mutters, earning a grunt of agreement from Mattia.

Rafe snorts, though the look on his face makes it clear he's missing his own piece right now. We're both unarmed, exactly like the rules demand. It's not a comfortable position to be in.

"Let's get this shit over with," I growl.

Antonio and Mattia exit the vehicle first to make sure everything is copacetic. They check around, looking in windows and under cars, prodding at bushes. Mattia vanishes inside the deli to look it over.

"I'm marrying Amalia," Rafe says.

"Figured as much." I arch a brow, asking the same question he asked me the other night. "Does she know?"

He gives me the finger, smirking. "She said yes, *stronzo*."

"*Congratulazioni*," I murmur, genuinely happy for him. *Merda*. He deserves happiness in his life. Perhaps more than any of us. He's held us together, no matter how steep the personal cost. And it has been steep. He sacrificed everything. "You deserve peace."

"So do you." He eyes me for a moment. "You and Gabriel have been trying to take our businesses legitimate for a long time. When this shit is over, you two should focus on that again."

I glance at him in surprise.

"I have Mattia," he says with a shrug. "You're a phone call away. Get her out of this world. She's been in it long enough."

"And Amalia hasn't?"

He smiles softly. "Amalia knows where she belongs."

I'm not sure what the fuck that means. I'm not sure I want to know. My brother's *regina* is a fierce woman, exactly what he needs to keep him busy.

Mattia exits the deli, signaling the *all clear*. Rafe and I exchange a glance and then climb out of the Bentayga.

"He's inside," Mattia mutters. "Enzo is with him."

"Not Marcello?" I ask. Enzo Gianni is one of their captains, a second or third cousin to Emilio. He's third in command after Marcello, definitely not the one who should be here now.

Mattia shakes his head.

Rafe and I exchange a glance. Why isn't Marcello here? Is there division in the ranks, or is this some sort of setup? Either one is equally possible at this point.

"Find Marcello," I mutter to Mattia. "I want to know where the fuck he is and why he isn't here."

"Will do," Mattia says.

I spear a look at Antonio. "You call Alessio. Make sure he knows that Marcello isn't here and to keep his eyes peeled."

Antonio nods.

"Leave a gun on the bench while Enzo pats me down." I glance at Rafe. "You distract Emilio so he doesn't see him leaving it."

"You think it's a setup," Rafe says.

"You don't? Marcello isn't here for a reason. I'm guessing Callandria is the reason. They're going after her," I growl, my temper rising. Emilio Genovese better pray to God I'm wrong. Not even heaven itself will keep her from me. Her father and brother certainly won't. She's mine.

"Slip him the gun," Rafe says to Antonio. "*Cazzo*, Luca. Just don't fucking kill him."

I make no promises.

Rafe curses again and pulls the door open. A blast of air hits me in the face, carrying the stench of stale cigar smoke. *Cristo*. I don't know why they insist on smoking the damn things. The inside of the deli is dimly lit, the blinds drawn. The place no longer functions, though it has all the trappings, down to fresh ingredients in the kitchen. *La Cosa Nostra* is good at keeping up appearances.

Emilio and Enzo stand in the center of the room, dressed in matching dark blue suits. Emilio turns in our direction, casting a cold, contemptuous look over us. Unlike his daughter, there's no fire in his eyes, only coldness. He's a giant of a man, as thick as he is tall. A glimpse of who Marcello will be twenty-five years from now, perhaps.

Enzo is a handsome bastard, rising through the ranks only because Genovese blood runs through his veins and he has no conscience. He kills with no remorse, steals with no regret. He's a soulless sycophant.

"Valentino," Emilio says, inclining his head to Rafe in the barest show of respect. His gaze flicks to me. "Luca."

"Genovese," Rafe says, his voice cold. "Enzo." He casts a glance over his shoulder at Mattia. "Search him."

Emilio grunts but doesn't object as Mattia steps forward. He pats Emilio down carefully, checking him for weapons. Once he's satisfied, he steps back, nodding to Rafe.

"Let's get on with it then," Rafe says.

"Not so fast. Not until Enzo searches the two of you."

Rafe rolls his eyes. "We don't make a habit of violating our oaths, Genovese. But since you insist." He steps forward impatiently, his arms spread.

Antonio shifts toward the bench beside me, moving casually.

Enzo quickly pats Rafe down, finding nothing.

"Your turn," Emilio spits at me.

I resist the urge to plant my fist in his face and step forward, moving to block Antonio from view.

Enzo grabs my arms, carefully feeling for a weapon. He's thorough, I'll give him that.

"Was Marcello too busy to join us, Genovese?" Rafe asks, stepping in front of Emilio to distract him. "Isn't he your second-in-command, or did I miss some memo?"

"You missed nothing, Valentino. My son had other matters to attend to today."

"Nothing pressing, I hope."

"It was a family matter," Emilio lies. "I'm sure you understand how important those can be."

"Of course," Rafe says, his voice flat.

Enzo elbows me in the dick, intentionally, I'm sure.

"*Stronzo*," I mutter.

He grabs my balls.

"Those are my balls," I growl. "Would you like me to drop my pants so you can see what a real pair looks like, or are you done grabbing on them now?"

His expression sours, hatred flashing in his eyes, but he releases my dick and quickly pats down my legs before rising to his feet again.

"They're clean," he mutters.

"Satisfied?" Rafe asks Emilio, who nods. "Good. Enzo, Antonio, get the fuck out."

I quickly slide onto the bench, feeling for the weapon Antonio left for me. My hand closes over it. I tuck it under my jacket, hiding it from view. If Emilio tries anything, we'll be ready.

Enzo and Antonio file out, followed by Mattia, who takes up a position in front of the doors. As Rafe's consigliere, he'd usually stay inside, but since Emilio hasn't chosen a consigliere yet and we killed Battista, he'll guard the doors. Enzo doesn't get to stay. Neither does Antonio.

In truth, I wouldn't have brought him at all, but Rafe wanted to remind Emilio that my position is secure. Emilio is the one on shaky ground. He has no consigliere and he's losing votes by the day. If he chooses war, he chooses death for everyone. An alliance is his best choice.

"Take a seat, Genovese," Rafe says, motioning for Emilio to slide into the booth across from me.

Emilio chafes at being told what to do but reluctantly settles onto the bench to scowl at me.

Rafe waits until he's seated to slide in next to me. "You demanded this meeting, so talk, Genovese. Why are we here?"

"I want my daughter back from this *pezzo di merda*," he growls, jabbing a finger in my direction. "She'll marry into your family over my dead body."

"That can be arranged," I offer.

"Despite how she's acting, she's a Genovese!"

"What the fuck does that mean?" I ask, my voice dangerously soft.

"You know exactly what I mean, Valentino," he says, his face contorting with disgust. "She's a *principessa*, not your plaything. God only knows what lies you filled her head with to get her to act like your little *zoccola*."

I slam my fist down on the tabletop. "Say whatever you want to say about me, Genovese," I snarl. "But insult her again and I'll rip your goddamn tongue out."

"Do not tell me what I can and cannot do with my own daughter!" he bellows, rising to his feet. "You two may rule this city but you have no control over my family or how I choose to run it."

"Watch your fucking tone, Genovese," Rafe snaps at him.

"Or what? You'll murder me in cold blood like you did my father?" Spittle flies from the corners of Emilio's mouth. "*Nessuno mi unfungulo*. Prove you have honor left and release my daughter."

"You want to talk to us about honor?" Rafe growls. "You sold your daughter into a marriage contract before she was out of diapers!"

"As is my right."

"She doesn't agree."

"She's too young to know what she wants," Emilio says. "If she did, she wouldn't be sharing his bed. She'd have a little respect for herself and this family."

"If you insult her again, I'm not going to stop him when he breaks your jaw," Rafe warns him.

"Don't pretend you care, Valentino," Emilio says. "You two may have her fooled, but we all know the only reason she's in his bed is to punish us for what my father did to your *regina*."

"At least you admit Tommaso Genovese was a piece of shit," Rafe growls.

"It takes one to recognize one, yes?"

"I said watch your fucking tone!" Rafe snaps, pounding his fist against the table hard enough to rattle it on the base. "I'm still the *Capo dei capi*, Genovese. Disrespect me again, and I'll teach you precisely what that means."

He's intentionally pushing us. He wants us to react. He wants to keep us here, screaming at each other for as long as possible. The realization hits me like a freight train.

Why? What is he trying to accomplish?

Callandria. Of course. He's trying to give Marcello time to get Callandria out of there. Except he's not nearly as smart as he thinks he is. The stench of desperation covers him. He needs Callandria back, not because she's his daughter, not because he'd rather die than see her married to a Valentino, but because his plans hinge on having her under his control.

"Enough," I growl, done wasting time with this bullshit game of his. "Cut the bullshit, Emilio. What did you do?"

"*Va' a farti fottere*," he spits at me, refusing to answer.

"Even if Marcello gets to her, she won't leave with him. She's where she wants to be."

He turns those cold eyes on me, smiling in a way that makes my fucking soul shrivel. "Then you don't know my daughter well, Valentino. As soon as Marcello tells her that your life depends on her leaving with him, she'll walk out of there without hesitation. She'll marry Andrea Maceo and you'll never see her again."

Figlio di puttana. He thinks he can take her from me? Give her to some other man? Is that what this is about? He needs her to wed Maceo? I roar in denial, in fury, rising to my feet so quickly I flip the table.

"Andrea Maceo will put his ring on her finger over my dead body," I growl, pacing toward Emilio. "I'll rip this goddamn city to the ground before I let that happen."

Panic lights Emilio's eyes. He scrambles backward, reaching into a planter along a low shelf, trying to get his hands on what I can only assume is a weapon.

"Watch out!" Rafe shouts to me, making the same connection.

I don't think about it.

I don't even hesitate.

I raise the gun in my hand and pull the trigger, my field of vision red with rage.

Emilio bellows in pain, but I'm already running, racing as fast as I can to go.

No one is taking Callandria from me. *No one.*

Chapter Eleven

CALLANDRIA

"Marcello," I whisper, pleading with him for the thousandth time since he brought me back to my father's house. I don't know where my mother is, but she isn't here. I think they sent her away. They're preparing for war. "You have to listen to me. We can pay whatever debt he owes to the Maceo family, but you can't let him go through with this! You have to convince him to let me go. Luca will kill everyone if you don't."

"And that's the kind of man you want to spend your life with, Callie? One willing to destroy your family?" Marcello asks, watching me from a leather wingback chair across the room, a gun on his lap.

"You mean one trying to protect me from the people determined to hurt me?" I ask, pacing in circles around the living room. It's odd. I spent my whole life in this house, but it's never felt as much like home to me as Luca's does after a matter of days. Every piece of furniture in it is worth a small fortune, but it's all cold and unwelcoming, especially now. I want to be back at Luca's in his arms so badly. There's warmth there, and laughter.

Please, survive. Please, don't let this be the end, I pray, fighting the hopelessness beating in my chest. I can't give up. Luca wouldn't. He'd fight until the end. He'd fight for me.

"*Cristo*, Callie," Marcello says, staring at me likes he's never seen me before. "What happened to you?"

"What happened to me?" I laugh abruptly, a sharp, abrasive sound I hardly recognize. "I grew up in this house, Marcello! At thirteen, I told my father I wanted to go to college someday. He laughed in my face and told me that I'd never do that. That I was marrying Andrea Maceo on my twenty-first birthday and I didn't have a choice. That it was what was *required* of me as a *principessa*. When I pleaded, he sent me to my room for a week! Princesses smile and serve the family with pride. They don't act like selfish brats, he said. I've spent every day since dreading my twenty-first birthday! That's what happened to me!"

"*Dio*," Marcello mutters.

"And then I finally find a way out. I'm finally free. I find a way to protect our family and forge an alliance while snatching a little bit of happiness for myself, and you drag me right back to my own personal hell," I cry. "You act like Luca is a monster, but he's the only person who has *ever* cared what I want."

"Callie, that's not true."

"Yes, it is," I sob. "He could have forced me to his bed, Marcello. He could have taken what he wanted. He didn't. He's been nothing but good to me. He's treated me like family. And he's done everything possible to make sure no one else pays for what our grandfather did. He doesn't want a war. He doesn't want the Genovese territory. He just wants me! It's my own family who want to use me, even when they know that doing it is killing me."

My brother is silent for a moment and then he shoves a hand through his dark hair, ruffling it. "You really believe that, don't you?"

"I don't believe it," I whisper, wiping my eyes. "I know it. I think about marrying Andrea Maceo, and I would rather die. If that's what the future holds for me, just end it now, Marcello. Don't drag out my death. Kill me now."

I don't love Andrea Maceo. I don't even like him. My skin crawls when I think about him touching me or sharing my bed. He's a monster just like his father. He takes and takes and takes until there's nothing left.

"Luca loves me, Marcello. So much he'll risk everything to set me free, even his own life. That's the future I choose. That's the man I choose." I swallow, trembling. "And if you love me at all, you'll let me go. Please."

If Luca's alive right now, he's on his way here. He'll kill everyone to get to me or die trying. Marcello has to let me go before that happens.

"Fuck," Marcello mutters, striding across the room toward me. He snatches me into his arms, pulling me into a fierce hug. "You better not be wrong about him, *sorella*. If he hurts you, I'll tear their empire down with my bare hands."

I sob, my knees threatening to buckle as relief crashes through me. He's letting me go. *Dio Santo*, he's letting me—

Pow. Pow. Pow.

I scream as gunfire erupts outside, so close it sounds as if it's right on top of us.

"*Cazzo!*" Marcello shouts, dragging me to the floor as chaos erupts outside.

Enforcers shout, a mix of Italian and English that makes it clear they're under attack. Another gunshot rings out.

"Luca," I sob, fighting to get free of Marcello's embrace. "Luca!"

"*Calmati! Calmati*!" Marcello growls, shaking me gently. "I'll handle it. You stay here. Don't move from this spot, Callie."

I sob again, nodding as he pulls away and scrambles toward the door. More guards pour out of the back of the house, rushing toward the patio doors with guns drawn.

I bite my lip, holding back a scream of fury. This is my worst nightmare in the flesh, and Marcello expects me to just sit here and wait. No. I won't.

I push myself to my feet and race toward the front door. Marcello left it standing open. It's eerily quiet outside now. Too quiet.

My feet fly down the steps.

I shudder in horror at the bodies of my father's guards littering the ground. How did Luca kill so many so quickly? *Dio*. He's truly on the warpath.

I race around the corner of the house to see a vision that rivals my worst nightmares. Luca is alive, but my father's guards have half a dozen guns pointed at his back. And he has his aimed at Marcello's head.

"You took her from me," Luca snarls, his expression thunderous. Murderous fury dancing like lightning in his eyes. "You tried to give her to another man."

"She's inside, Valentino," Marcello says, speaking softly. He has his hands raised. "She's safe."

"I should kill you right here and now," Luca snaps.

"No!" I cry, throwing myself in front of Marcello.

My father's guards shift uneasily.

"*Bella*," Luca breathes.

"*Calmati*!" Marcello snaps at the men behind Luca. "Lower your weapons."

They hesitate.

"*Adesso*!" Marcello growls. "If anyone fucking shoots my sister, you'll wish for death."

All six reluctantly lower their weapons.

"Luca," I sob, tears rolling down my face. "It's over, Luca. Please take me home."

He hesitates, clearly torn between his desire to punish my brother and his need to give me what I want. That battle plays out across his handsome face, etching it in stark lines of agony.

"Please," I whisper. "He was letting me go. He wasn't going to turn me over to Andrea."

A menacing snarl rips from his lips when I say Andrea's name. And then I understand.

"I belong to you." I step toward him, my hands outstretched. "Body, heart, and soul. *Sempre*."

He roars, rushing forward to scoop me up. His strong arms surround me, holding me close as his lips slant down over mine, staking his claim on me in my father's driveway. I cling to him, tears spilling down my cheeks as the vise around my heart shatters and falls away.

And for the first time in hours, perhaps for the first time since I was thirteen, I breathe freely.

Chapter Twelve

LUCA

"*Bella*," I whisper, pressing adoring kisses all over Callandria's perfect face as we lay in our bed, holding each other close. As soon as we arrived home, I carried her upstairs. Rafe already sent Ricardo and Alessio off to get medical attention. They're going to be all right, though it's going to be a rough recovery for both of them. Ricardo has a concussion. Marcello's knife nicked Alessio's lung. They'll both be down for a while. But they'll survive.

Callandria wept with relief when I gave her the news. It seems she has a soft spot for the old man and her bodyguard. I'm trying very hard not to be jealous of that fact. I don't want to share a single piece of her heart with another man, but it seems I'll be sharing it with a few of them. It'll drive me fucking crazy. I'll be possessive and jealous and have my cock down her throat and my tongue buried in her cunt, making her scream my name at every available opportunity to remind myself that she's mine and only mine. But I'll learn to live with it.

If it makes her happy, I'll learn.

"*Bella principessa. Sei tutto per me.*"

"You're everything to me too," she whispers, nuzzling her face against my jaw. "I was so afraid I was going to lose you today, Luca." Her eyes grow damp. "I can't lose you. *Sei la mia anima gemella.*"

You're my twin soul.

"You are my soul, *piccolina*."

"No," she says, shaking her head. "I've seen your soul, Luca. I've felt it. It's bright and fierce."

"So are you, Callandria."

"You make me feel that way."

"You are that way." I kiss a trail down her chest, laving the flat of my tongue across the hard bud of her nipple. "So bright." I sink my teeth into the taut flesh and then suck hard. "So fierce."

"Luca," she moans, thrusting her hand into my hair and pulling.

I growl, my dick raging to life. Fuck. Even now, I want in her. Especially now. I'm a possessive, jealous asshole. Part of me is still furious that her father and Marcello tried to take her from me to give her to another man. Part of me wants to hunt Andrea Maceo down and kill him slowly. The only reason he's still breathing is because Marcello swore he had no knowledge of Emilio's decision.

Emilio has been borrowing money from Alessandro Maceo against the marriage contract for years, trying to keep himself afloat until Callandria and Andrea wed. He's in deep. Far deeper than the bastard can afford. It's a problem.

I groan and regretfully roll off of Callandria, pulling her up against my side.

"You stopped," she says, pouting.

"Only for a little while, *bella*." I smile, smoothing the wrinkle from her forehead. "We need to talk."

She sighs quietly. "Did you kill him?"

"No." I pause. "But I shot him in the leg."

"He deserved it," she whispers fiercely. "He was going to kill you."

"I know." I press my lips to her forehead. "He told me right before I shot him."

"Why didn't you kill him?"

It's a good question. I wanted to do it. Had he been anyone else, I wouldn't have hesitated to do it, but... "Because I don't want you to spend the rest of your life waking up next to the man who murdered your father," I admit. "It would haunt you and poison us. I won't allow his death to stand between us, *piccolina*."

I want to be a man worthy of her, one she can look at with pride. I'd never be that had I taken his life. Some part of her still loves him, even though he doesn't deserve it. If keeping him alive keeps her in my arms, then I'll make it my personal mission to keep the motherfucker breathing.

"Thank you," she whispers.

"There's nothing I wouldn't do for you, Callandria. That's what it means to love a *principessa, bella*. That's what it means to be a man worthy of the love of one."

"You're worthy."

I smile against her temple, glad she thinks so.

"You said the rest of my life."

"Hmm?"

"You said you don't want me to spend the rest of my life waking up next to the man who murdered my father," she says.

I tilt her face up until her amber eyes meet mine. "I'll give you your freedom, *bella*, but I can't let you go. Don't ask it of me. You're the reason I breathe."

"Then marry me, Luca." She crawls onto my lap, straddling my thighs. "Let's make this alliance binding so no one can try to come between us again."

Dio. How can I say no to that? Why would I when it's exactly what I want?

"As you command," I breathe, cupping the back of her head and dragging her mouth down to mine for a scorching kiss. I pour myself into it, giving her everything I have, my heart, my soul, my life. Every piece of me belongs to her anyway.

"What happens now?" she asks when I roll her to her back. "With my family, I mean."

"It's up to you."

"I think we should throw our support behind Marcello."

I lean up on my elbow to stare down at her in surprise. "Really?

She bites her lip, nodding. "He doesn't want the job. It seems to me like that makes him the best man to do it. I trust him, Luca. We can trust an alliance we build with him. I won't ever trust my father again."

"Then Marcello it is."

"Just like that, huh?"

"Ah, *bella*," I say, chuckling as I kiss a trail across her belly. "It's never just like that. But when you run the city, you make the rules. And in case you've forgotten, we run the city."

"Lucky us," she breathes, arching toward my mouth.

"For once, I'm inclined to agree. Now hush, *bella*. I have work to do."

The chains clink as I drag them onto the bed, reaching for her wrists.

"Luca," she moans, her eyes dilating with desire.

"You owe me an heir." I reach for her wrists. "While you're coming all over my cock and screaming my name,

I plan on collecting what you owe tonight. So be a good little princess and give me what I want, *bella*."

"Yes," she whispers. "God, yes, Luca."

Epilogue

CALLANDRIA

Five Years Later

"Luca," I moan, running my thumbs over my nipples as I drop down on his cock, riding him hard. Sweat drips down my body and soaks my hair. My lungs burn from exertion, but I've never felt better.

"*Cazzo, bella,*" my husband growls, the chains rattling as he fights against them, staring up at me with that look in his eyes. The one that tells me someone is going to pay for this.

I already know it'll be me. That's the entire reason I chained him to the bed while he slept. Nothing pisses him off more than not being able to touch me when he wants.

And nothing makes me hotter than when he finally gets his hands on me.

"You feel so good," I moan, pinching my nipples. "Feel how I take you, Luca." I lean forward, putting my mouth close to his ear. "I'm such a good little princess for you, aren't I?"

He growls, his upper body tensing as he yanks hard against the chains. The ring in the wall groans and then rips free, flying like a missile across the room.

I squeak in shock…and then I'm on my back with his hand around my throat.

"You want to play, bella?" he growls, pinning me to the bed beneath him as he slams into me in one deep thrust. "You want to make me crazy?"

"Yes," I moan, not denying it. He wouldn't believe me even if I did. After five years, he knows exactly how my mind works. He knows what I want and what I need, often before I do. And he spends hours giving it to me. When the twins go down for the night, it's his turn to play.

"Then take it, you filthy little princess," he snarls, clamping his free hand over my mouth to stifle my screams as he gives me exactly what I wanted. He fucks me hard, his hand tight around my throat.

I claw at his arms, screaming in ecstasy as he builds me up and knocks me down twice in rapid succession. The third time, I manage to pry his hand away from my mouth.

"I'm pregnant!" I cry, my body bowing to his again. Waves crash over me, dragging me under. Somehow, I manage to keep my eyes open.

His eyes widen in shock as my confession registers. He curses, his body locking up as he follows me over the edge.

"*Merda*," he groans, quickly rolling off me. "Get these fucking chains off me, *bella. Adesso.*"

Crap. He's mad. Maybe I shouldn't have chained him up and told him in the middle of an orgasm. But it seemed only fair since I'm positive that's exactly how I ended up pregnant again. It's how I ended up pregnant with the twins, too.

I sit up and unbind his wrists.

"Please don't be—"

He hits me like a bullet, scooping me up into his arms. "*Bella*," he breathes, spinning me in circles and laughing. "*Bella principessa*. You're pregnant? *Cristo*. You're pregnant!"

I sob, tears spilling over to run down my cheeks. "We're pregnant, Luca."

I may carry the babies, but he's there every step of the way. When I was pregnant five years ago, he was incredible. He took such good care of me and our babies. He took care of everything.

By the time the twins arrived, he and Marcello had hammered out the details of an alliance between the Genovese and Valentino family, paid off my father's debts to the

Maceos, and secured the Genovese throne for Marcello. My father wasn't thrilled to lose the power, but by then, no one really cared what he had to say. Luca himself had a better chance of being voted in than my father once word leaked—with Luca's help—that he'd tried to force me into a marriage I didn't want to save his own miserable neck.

My mother didn't speak to him for a year. He's tried to make amends since the twins were born, but I'm not ready to forgive him yet. I'm not sure if I ever will be. I allow him to see them only with supervision. And I never see him alone, either. He hurt me to save himself. Now that I have kids, I understand even less how he could do it. I no longer try. It's his burden and his shame to live with.

Alessandro Maceo apologized to me a few years ago. He said he never should have agreed to the contract. And he was sorry that it had come at such a high price for me. I'm not sure if he meant it. His family isn't exactly known for being scrupulous or moral, but Luca and Rafe keep a close eye on him. I don't think we have to worry about anyone else being forced into a marriage they don't want while the Valentino family is in charge. They've made it clear where they stand on the issue and what the consequences will be.

I'm free...or as free as I can be married to Luca Valentino. He has no expectations of me. I do what I want and go where I want so long as Alessio accompanies me, and I don't endanger myself. I've been taking college courses.

I volunteer at a soup kitchen. And I sleep peacefully at night. I breathe easy.

We didn't merely stop a war. We built a future. I've never been happier.

Luca places me back in the bed, crawling over me. "*Ti amo, bella*," he whispers, his eyes bright. And I know he feels it too. Happiness. Joy. Hope. The man who once told me he was never happy finally knows peace too.

"*Ti amo*, Luca," I breathe, pulling him down for a kiss. "*Sempre.*"

Author's Note

Thanks so much for reading Wanton! If you enjoyed the book, please consider leaving a review!

Wicked, Gabriel's book, will be coming in the spring of 2023! Nico's book, Physical Science, and Rafe's book, Wrecked, are out now!

Want more mafia romance from me? Snow's Prince, a Silver Spoon Underworld story, releases on February 7th!

Snow's Prince

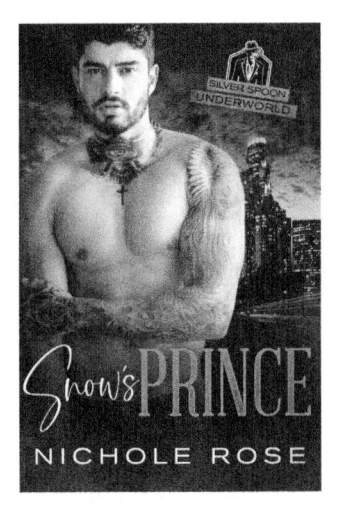

When Dimitri Arakas infiltrated the cartel moving in on Silver Spoon Falls, his only plan was to find the boss and take him out. He never expected to discover a woman running things. Nor did he expect to be sent to kill her stepdaughter. He certainly didn't plan to rescue the curvy little princess from her evil stepmother. Now, he's got a pissed off cartel out for his head, the woman of his dreams hiding out in his house…and her seven suspicious furry companions making his life all kinds of complicated. Sorting this out is going to be a nightmare. But hey, no one ever said a life of crime was easy.

A new "family" is coming to Silver Spoon Falls, TX.

The well-known Arakas men are looking to expand their operations, and the small Texas town is the perfect place to start a new, less-than-above-board business venture. Along the way, the dangerous, wealthy men are going to find a whole lot of trouble…and the sassy women who will bring the possessive crime bosses to their knees. This family will turn the town on its ear looking for their curvy soulmates. Prince Charming's crown may be a little tarnished in this spin-off series of sweet and steamy mafia instalove romances, but these possessive bad boys always put their women first.

Don't worry, Nichole and Loni like to keep things light. Come along with us on this wild, steamy ride.

You've already fallen for the Silver Spoon MC. Now get ready to fall for the Silver Spoon Underworld!

Snow's Prince is coming soon. Pre-order live!

Nichole's Book Beauties

Want to connect with Nichole and other readers? We're building a girl gang! Join Nichole Rose's Book Beauties on Facebook for fun, games, and behind-the-scenes exclusives!

Instalove Book Club

The Instalove Book Club is now in session!

Get the inside scoop from your favorite instalove authors, meet new authors to love, and snag freebies and bonus content from featured authors every month. The Instalove Book Club newsletter goes out once per week!

Join now to get your hands on bonus scenes and brand-new, exclusive content from our first six featured authors.

Join the Club: http://instalovebookclub.com

Follow Nichole

Sign-up for Nichole's mailing list at http://authornicholerose.com/newsletter to stay up to date on all new releases and for exclusive ARC giveaways from Nichole Rose.

Want to connect with Nichole and other readers? Join Nichole Rose's Book Beauties on Facebook!

facebook.com/AuthorNicholeRose/

instagram.com/AuthorNicholeRose

twitter.com/AuthNicholeRose

bookbub.com/authors/nichole-rose

tiktok.com/@authornicholerose

More By Nichole Rose

Her Alpha Series
Her Alpha Daddy Next Door
Her Alpha Boss Undercover
Her Alpha's Secret Baby
Her Alpha Protector
Her Date with an Alpha
Her Alpha: The Complete Series

Her Bride Series
His Future Bride
His Stolen Bride
His Secret Bride
His Curvy Bride
His Captive Bride

His Blushing Bride
His Bride: The Complete Series

Claimed Series
Possessing Liberty
Teaching Rowan
Claiming Caroline
Kissing Kennedy
Claimed: The Complete Series

Love on the Clock Series
Adore You
Hold You
Keep You
Protect You
Love on the Clock: The Complete Series

The Billionaires' Club
The Billionaire's Big Bold Weakness
The Billionaire's Big Bold Wish
The Billionaire's Big Bold Woman
The Billionaire's Big Bold Wonder

Playing for Keeps
Cutie Pie

Ice Breaker

Ice Prince

Ice Giant

The Second Generation
A Blushing Bride for Christmas

Love Bites
Come Undone

Dripping Pearls

Silver Spoon MC
The Surgeon

The Heir

The Lawyer

The Prodigy

The Bodyguard

Silver Spoon MC Collection: Nichole's Crew

Echoes of Forever

His Christmas Miracle
Taken by the Hitman
Wicked Saint

The Ruined Trilogy
Physical Science
Wrecked
Wanton

Destination Romance
Romancing the Cowboy
Beach House Beauty

Standalone Titles
A Touch of Summer
Black Velvet
His Secret Obsession
Dirty Boy
Naughty Little Elf
Tempted by December
Devil's Deceit
A Bride for the Beast (writing with Fern Fraser)

Easy on Me
Easy Ride
Easy Surrender

One Night with You
Falling Hard
Model Behavior
Learning Curve
Angel Kisses

Silver Spoon Falls
Xavier's Kitten
Callum's Hope

writing with Loni Ree as Loni Nichole
Dillon's Heart
Razor's Flame
Ryker's Reward
Zane's Rebel
Grizz's Passion (coming soon)

About Nichole Rose

Nichole Rose writes filthy, feel-good romance for curvy readers. Her books feature headstrong, sassy women and the alpha males who consume them. From grumpy detectives to country boys with attitude to instalove and over-the-top declarations, nothing is off-limits.

Nichole is sure to have a steamy, sweet story just right for everyone. She fully believes the world is ugly enough without trying to fit falling in love into a one-size-fits-all box.

When not writing, Nichole enjoys fine wine, cute shoes, and everything supernatural. She is happily married to the love of her life and is a proud mama to the world's most ridiculous fur-babies. She and her husband live in the Pacific Northwest.

You can learn more about Nichole and her books at authornicholerose.com.

facebook.com/AuthorNicholeRose/

instagram.com/AuthorNicholeRose

twitter.com/AuthNicholeRose

bookbub.com/authors/nichole-rose

tiktok.com/@authornicholerose